TIME

Writings from an Unbound Europe

GENERAL EDITOR

Andrew Wachtel

EDITORIAL BOARD

Clare Cavanagh

Michael Henry Heim

Roman Koropeckyj

Ilya Kutik

■ □ ■ □ ■

ZORAN ŽIVKOVIĆ

TIME GIFTS

Translated from the Serbian by Alice Copple-Tošić

NORTHWESTERN UNIVERSITY PRESS

EVANSTON, ILLINOIS

Northwestern University Press
Evanston, Illinois 60208-4210

Originally published in Serbian in 1997 under the title *Vremenski darovi*.
Copyright © 1997 by Zoran Živković. English translation copyright
© 2000 by Northwestern University Press. Published 2000 by
Northwestern University Press. All rights reserved.

Printed in the United States of America

ISBN 0-8101-1781-9 (CLOTH)
ISBN 0-8101-1782-7 (PAPER)

Library of Congress Cataloging-in-Publication Data

Živković, Zoran.
 [Vremenski darovi. English]
 Time gifts / Zoran Živković ; translated from the Serbian by
Alice Copple-Tošić.
  p. cm. — (Writings from an unbound Europe)
 ISBN 0-8101-1781-9 (alk. paper) — ISBN 0-8101-1782-7 (pbk. : alk. paper)
 I. Title. II. Series.
PG1419.36.I954 V7413 2000
891.8'2354—dc21   00-008926

The paper used in this publication meets the minimum requirements of
the American National Standard for Information Sciences—Permanence
of Paper for Printed Library Materials, ANSI Z39.48-1984.

To the dear misanthrope

CONTENTS

The Astronomer 3

The Paleolinguist 23

The Watchmaker 43

The Artist 65

GIFTS

THE ASTRONOMER

I

HE HAD TO ESCAPE FROM THE MONASTERY.

He should not be there at all; he had never wanted to become a monk. He'd said that to his father, but his father had been unrelenting, as usual, and his mother did not have the audacity to oppose him, even though she knew that her son's inclinations and talents lay elsewhere. The monks had treated him badly from the beginning. They had abused and humiliated him, forced him to do the dirtiest jobs, and when their nocturnal visits commenced he could stand it no longer.

He set off in flight, and a whole throng of pudgy, unruly brothers started after him, screaming hideously, torches and mantles raised, certain he could not get away. His legs became heavier and heavier as he attempted to reach the monastery gate, but it seemed to be deliberately withdrawing, becoming more distant at every step.

And then, when they had just about reached him, the monks suddenly stopped in their tracks. Their obscene shouts all at once turned into frightened screams of distress. They began to cross themselves feverishly, pointing to something in front of him, but all he could see there was the wide-open gate and the clear night sky stretching beyond it. The gate no longer retreated before him, and once again he felt light and fast.

He was filled with tremendous relief when he reached the arched vault of the great gate. He knew they could no longer reach him, that he had gotten away. He stepped outside to meet the stars, but his foot did not alight on solid ground as it should have. It landed on something soft and squishy, and he started to sink as though he'd stepped in quicksand. He flailed his arms but could find no support.

He realized what he had fallen into by the terrible stench. It was the deep pit at the bottom of the monastery walls; the cooks threw the unusable entrails of slaughtered animals into it every day through a small, decayed wooden door. The cruel priests often threatened the terrified boy that he, too, would end up there if he did not satisfy their aberrant desires. The pit certainly should not have been located at the entrance to the holy edifice, but this utmost sacrilege for some reason seemed neither strange nor unfitting.

He began to sink rapidly into the thick tangle of bloated intestines, and when they almost reached his shoulders he became terror stricken. Just a few more moments and he would sink completely into this slimy morass. Unable to do anything else, he raised his desperate eyes, and there, illuminated by the reflection of the distant torches, he saw the silhouette of a naked, bony creature squatting on the edge of the pit, looking at him maliciously and snickering.

He did not see the horns and tail, but even without these marks he had no trouble understanding who it was; now that it was too late, he realized whom the terrified monks had seen. He instinctively froze at this pernicious stare, suddenly wanting to disappear as soon as possible under the slimy surface and hide there. All at once the blood and stench stopped making him nauseous; now they seemed precious, like the last refuge before the most terrible of all fates.

And truly, when he had plunged completely into that watery substance, it turned out that it was not, after all, the discarded entrails of pigs, sheep, and goats, as it had seemed, but was a mother's womb, soft and warm. He curled up in it, knees under his chin, as endless bliss filled his being. No one could do anything to him here; he was safe, protected.

The illusion of paradise was not allowed to last very long, however. Demonic eyes, like a sharp awl, quickly pierced through the layers of extraneous flesh and reached his tiny crouched being. He tried to withdraw before them, going even deeper into the womb, to the very bottom, but his persecutor did not give up. The thin membrane that surrounded his refuge burst the moment he leaned his back against it, having nowhere else to go, and he fell out—into reality.

And with him, out of his dream, came the eyes that continued their piercing stare.

He could not see them in the almost total darkness, but their immaterial touch was almost palpable. Suddenly awake, he realized that someone else was with him in the cell. He had not heard him come in, even though the door squeaked terribly, since probably no one had thought to oil it in years. How strange for him to fall into such a deep sleep; the night before their execution, only the toughest criminals managed to sleep. They were not burdened by their conscience or the thought of impending death, and he certainly was not one of them.

He raised his head a bit and looked around, confused. Although he felt he was not alone, his heart started racing when he saw the shape of a large man sitting on the bare boards of the empty bed across from him. If not for the light from the weakly burning torch in the hall that slanted into the cell through a narrow slit in the iron-plated door, he would not have been able to see him at all. As it was, all he could make out clearly were the pale hands folded in his lap, while his head was completely in the shadows, as though missing.

He asked himself in wonder whom it could be. A priest, by all judgments. They were the only ones allowed to visit prisoners before they were taken to be executed. Had the hour struck already? He quickly looked up at the high window with its rusty bars, but there was no sign of daybreak. The night was pitch black, without moonlight, so the opening was shown only as a slightly paler rectangle of darkness compared to the interior of the cell.

He knew they would not take him to the stake before dawn, and so he stared at the immobile figure uncertainly. Why had he come already? Would they be burning him earlier, perhaps, before the rabble gathered? But that made no sense. It was for this senseless multitude that they organized the public execution of heretics, to show in the most impressive manner what awaited those who dared come into conflict with catechism. The sight of the condemned, his body tied or nailed to the stake, writhing in terrible agony while around him darted the fiery tongues of flame, had a truly discouraging effect on even the boldest and most rebellious souls.

Or maybe this was a final effort to try to get him to renounce his discovery. That would be the best outcome for the church, of course, but he did not have the slightest intention of helping it; on the contrary, had he come this far just to give up now? If that was what was going on, their efforts were in vain.

"You had a bad dream," said the unseen head.

The voice was unfamiliar. It was not someone he had already met during the investigation and trial. It sounded gentle, but this might easily be a trick. He was well acquainted with the hypocrisy of priests. His worst problems had been with those who seemed understanding and helpful and then suddenly showed their pitiless faces.

"Why do you think that?" asked the prisoner, stretching numbly on the dirty, worn blanket that was his only bedding.

"I watched you twitch restlessly in your sleep."

"You watched me in the total darkness?"

"Eyes get accustomed to the dark if they are in it long enough and can see quite well there."

"There are eyes and eyes. Some get accustomed to it, others don't. I got here because I refused to get accustomed to the dark."

The fingers in the lap slowly interlaced, and the prisoner suddenly realized that they looked ghostly pale because he was wearing white gloves. They were part of the church dignitaries' vestments, which meant that the man in the cell with him was not an ordinary priest who had been sent to escort him to the stake. So, it was not time yet.

"Do you think that you will dispel the darkness with the brilliance of your fiery stake?" His tone was not cynical; it sounded more compassionate.

"I don't know. I couldn't think of any other way."

"It is also the most painful way. You have had the opportunity to witness death by burning at the stake, isn't that right?"

"Yes, of course. While I was at the monastery they took us several times to watch the execution of poor women accused of being witches. It is a compulsory part of the training of young monks, as you know. There is nothing like fear to inspire blind loyalty to the faith."

"Yes, fear is a powerful tool in the work of the church. But you, it seems, have remained unaffected by its influence?"

The prisoner rubbed his stiff neck. He could still somehow put up with the swill they fed him, the stale air and the humidity that surrounded him, and the constant squealing and scratching of hungry rodents that he'd been told were able to bite the ears and noses of heedless prisoners. But nothing had been so hard in this moldy prison as the fact that he did not have a pillow.

"What do you expect me to answer? That I'm not afraid of being burned? That I'm indifferent to the pain I'll soon be feeling at the stake? Only an imbecile would not be afraid."

"But you are not an imbecile. So why didn't you prevent such an end?"

"I had no choice."

"Of course you did. The only thing you were asked was to publicly renounce your conviction and repent, which is the most reasonable request of the court of the Inquisition when serious heretical sins are involved. If you had done that, you would have kept your title of royal astronomer and been allowed to continue teaching students."

"Who would attend the lectures of a royal astronomer who had renounced his discovery out of fear?"

"There is a question that comes before that. Why did you have to announce it in the first place? What did you want to achieve by that?"

"What should I have done—kept it a secret, all for myself?"

"You were aware that it goes counter to the teachings of Mother Church. You should have expected her to take all measures to protect herself."

"Of course I expected that. But I was relying on her hands being rather tied."

"It doesn't look like that, judging by the sentence you were given."

"Oh, you know perfectly well that the stake is not what the church wanted. It was a forced move after all attempts to talk me into cooperating failed."

"Based on your condition, I would not say that they tried all possible means. You do not look like someone who has been given the Inquisition's full treatment."

"Well, I'm not a witch. They didn't have to force me to agree to some meaningless accusation. I did not deny my guilt. That is why the whole investigation proceeded like some kind of friendly persuasion, even though, probably just to impress me, in the background stood the power of all the devices to mutilate, quarter, cut, break, and crush. But I was not even threatened with one of them, let alone put into any device. You do not torture someone who is valuable to you only as an ally. What good would it be if the royal astronomer were lame or blind?"

"Not even after the alliance has been irrevocably called off? The Inquisition can hardly boast of the virtues of forgiveness and compassion."

"That is why it is renowned for its patience and acumen. The sentence was made, but I have not been burned yet. There is still time. Attempts to win me over to the church's side will continue to the very end. In any case, that is why you are here, isn't it?"

There was an indistinct commotion from the end of the hall, followed by the sharp sound of a key unlocking a door and someone groaning painfully as he was thrown into the cell like a bag of potatoes. The Inquisition's investigators did their work primarily at night. The main room for the investigation was in the basement; in spite of the thick walls, horrible screams could be heard periodically, weakening the last remains of will and resistance in the other prisoners waiting for their turn to be taken down there. As they moved off after closing the door with a bang, one of the guards muttered something to the other, making him laugh raucously. For a long time his burst of laughter echoed like thunder through the stone hallway.

"But you, of course, will not relent?" asked the voice from the darkness after the echo finally died out.

"Of course."

"What is the real reason for that?"

"What do you mean?"

"You certainly are not a simpleminded idealist who has gotten involved in all this because you don't understand how the world works, what forces set it in motion. On the contrary, everything you have done from the beginning seems to have been carefully planned. You have lit a fire that only you can put out. It takes great resourcefulness to turn the tables on such an experienced service as the Inquisition, to tie its hands, as you say. And it takes the courage of a fanatic that is always lacking in idealists at the crucial moment, the readiness to go all the way, no matter what the cost. You, naturally, shy away from the pain that awaits you at the stake, but you will go to your execution nonetheless just because that will harm the church the most. What is it that she has done to you?"

The prisoner started to get up into a sitting position on the hard bed, feeling a stab of pain go all the way down his stiff back. As he did so, a scene from his dream suddenly rose to the surface of his memory. It was very vivid, although fixed, like some sort of ugly picture: the twisted faces of the monks lustfully reaching for his tiny, helpless body.

"Isn't it still early for my last confession?"

"I'm not here to listen to your confession."

"Oh, yes, it almost slipped my mind. You are here to prevail upon me to change my mind. But if you truly believe what you just said, it must be clear to you that it's impossible."

"It is clear to me."

"Then why are you wasting your time?"

There was no immediate reply from the other side of the cell. A hand rose from his lap and reached for something that was lying unseen on the wooden bench. A moment later it returned to the flickering shaft of light from the torch in the hall. It was now holding a slender black cane with a carved white figure on the top.

"I have more than enough time." The voice seemed to become muffled, more distant.

"But I don't. My hours are numbered."

"That's right. Soon they will come to take you to the stake, but before that you will be given one last chance to accept the church's offer. But, as we know, you will refuse. Although it makes no difference, really."

"It does make a difference. If I accept, everything I did will have been in vain."

"No, it won't. The damage was done the moment you announced your discovery, and it cannot be undone. The fluttering of the butterfly's wings should have been prevented before it initiated the storm. Even if the church made a sincere ally out of you, it would only slow down the harmful effects."

"Do you really think that this is sufficient to make me change my mind? I expected you to think of something more convincing."

"I have no intention of dissuading you. But that is the way things stand nonetheless. Heresy has been sown on fertile ground. Neither the stake nor repentance will turn your students away. They will start to spread forbidden knowledge, to add to it. Once set in motion, this course cannot be stopped, even though the Inquisition will undertake everything to obstruct it. You have let the genie out of the bottle, and he can no longer return to it. The church will finally realize this inexorability, but it will be too late then."

The prisoner strained to make out the hidden face in the impenetrable obscurity, but without success, even though his pupils were completely dilated.

"Isn't it unbecoming for a man of God to have so little faith in the future of the church?"

"Why do you think I am a man of God?"

A shroud of silence suddenly descended on the cell. Several long moments passed before the prisoner realized what was wrong. He had spent many nights alone in this place, and he could always hear some sort of noise: moaning from one of the neighboring cells, the screeching of rusty hinges, the murmur of the guards, muffled cries from the basement, the rustling of mice and rats, the creaking boards on which he lay, distant sounds of the outside world. Now all of that had mysteriously disappeared.

"Who are you?" he said, finally mustering the courage to break this silence of the tomb. The darkness did not answer; suddenly, once again the prisoner felt the stab of the piercing eyes that had followed him out of his dream. "The tempter?" The words were almost inaudible, so that he didn't know whether he said them or only thought them.

"Why should that bother you?" The voice remained just as gentle. "If I am the tempter, then we are on the same side. We have the same opponent."

"Why . . . why are you here? What do you want from me?" He had a strong urge to cross himself but at the last moment thought it somehow inappropriate.

"I don't want anything from you. On the contrary, I have a gift for you. Sort of a token of our alliance. A trip."

"A trip?"

"Don't worry, you won't leave this cell, and you will get back on time, before they come for you."

"What kind of a trip will it be if I stay here?"

"The only one possible under the circumstances: through time."

The prisoner blinked. This was not really happening. He was still asleep. However, there was no awakening that necessarily followed such a realization. He brought his hand to his face and pinched his cheek hard. The pain was real. Even too real.

"I don't want . . . to go . . . anywhere."

"But you'll like it there. I'm quite sure. The future has pleasant surprises for you."

"The future?"

"Yes. Almost three hundred years from now."

"Why would I want to go . . . to the future?"

"Out of curiosity, above all. Aren't you interested in checking whether you really succeeded in outwitting the church? Even though you certainly appear self-confident, there must still be a shadow of doubt inside. What if your sacrifice is in vain?"

"But you said it isn't. That my students . . ."

"A moment ago that did not sound convincing to you. In any case, can you believe in the word of the tempter, even when you're on the same side as he is?"

"What would the future corroborate? What would I see there?" As he asked these questions, he felt completely foolish. He had easily let himself be drawn into a crazy, impossible conversation. Where was the common sense he was so proud of? Had he gone out of his mind? He had heard that this sometimes happened to people waiting to be burned at the stake. Fear twisted their minds.

"A better question would be what you won't see. First of all, you won't see a monastery on the top of this hill. Its walls will still be there, but it will no longer contain dark, humid cells, corridors all sooty from torches, or a torture chamber in the basement."

"The monastery will fall to ruin?"

"No, it will be remodeled."

"What can you remodel a monastery into?"

The answer was preceded by brief silence that seemed to indicate a certain hesitation, indecision. "I suppose that in the end you would recognize it without my help, although it will certainly look . . . strange. But I would do well to prepare you. You will not have much time, and the future can have a stunning effect. At the time of your visit, instead of a monastery this will be an astronomical observatory."

He knew that he should say something in return, that it was expected of him, but he could not utter a word. His vocal cords were vibrating, forming confused questions, but his throat had closed completely at the top and no sound came out. He stared straight ahead blankly, his mouth empty.

In the infinite silence that reigned once again, a white-gloved hand put the cane between the knees, then disappeared in the folds of the black robe. The hand took a moment to find something there, then appeared with a round, flat object on the open palm. Golden reflections shone from its engraved curves. The dark figure's thumb moved along the edge of the object, and the lid popped open.

The hand extended toward the prisoner, but he remained stock-still. It was not indecision; the spasm that had closed his throat had now spread to his entire body. He wanted to move, do something, anything, he couldn't stay there motionless forever, but his muscles completely refused to obey.

"Yes, before you leave, there is one more thing you should know. It will please you, I believe. The observatory will be named after you."

The movement with which he accepted the watch had nothing to do with his will. It seemed to him that someone else received the tempter's gift, that he was just an observer who should indeed warn the incautious sinner not to do it, that it was insane. He wouldn't have listened, anyway, his soul was already lost, so it made no difference; actually, nothing could help him anymore.

The watch face radiated with a bright whiteness. In the dark cell it was a lighthouse summoning sailors, the flame of a candle attracting buzzing insects, a star luring the glass eye of the telescope. And over it were two ornate hands at a right angle, forming a large letter *L*.

II

Staring at the shiny surface, he failed to notice the changes that had started to take place. Something sparkled in the cell, apparitions passed through it more transparent than ghosts, and the specter from the other bed instantly dissolved into nothingness.

His attention was attracted only by the sudden daylight in the high barred window.

Isn't it still early? he asked himself, raising his eyes in bewilderment.

But the time of miracles had just begun. His eyes barely had time to twinkle before it was dark in the window again. The astronomer in him opened his mouth to contest the obvious, but he was silenced by the stronger voice of the child who cares not at all whether something is possible or not, as long as it is fascinating.

Many short interchanges of light and darkness took place before the child had had enough of this monotonous kaleidoscope, finally letting the scientist think about solving the mystery. There was only one explanation, of course. To accept it, however, one had to accept the impossible almost as an act of faith.

Before him the days and nights were passing at accelerated speed, but he could not ask the questions dictated by his reason. He had lost that right the moment he took the watch. In any event, was the "how" important? If this was the way to travel to the future, so be it.

Finally the hypnotic flashes of blue-gray and black images in the stone window tired even the astronomer. He turned around—and at first it seemed that the dizzy rush through time had stopped. Nothing was moving, everything looked fixed, unchanging. And then he realized that it was only an illusion. There could be no rapid changes here: the monastery walls were built to withstand the centuries.

Nonetheless, there were a few things in the cell made of less durable material. He stood transfixed as he watched the boards on the bed across from him gradually swell up from the perpetual humidity and then split and fall to the ground, where they slowly turned into a shapeless mass on the flagstones.

He jumped up from his bed when it struck him that the same fate had to happen to the boards on which he was sitting. Sure enough, they also ended up as a pile of sawdust. He, however, had not felt a thing: if this possibility had not crossed his mind, he would have continued to sit calmly on nothing, in midair.

The wooden door was considerably thicker, but in the end it, too, succumbed to the effects of decay. First the steel bars fell off, then the hinges gave way, cracks appeared, then gaps and holes, until finally there was nothing to stop him from going into the corridor. The cell ceased to be a prison. But on the other side of the threshold, freedom was an impenetrable darkness since no one lit torches to dispel it anymore.

Thoughts of freedom reminded him of the many prisoners who must have sojourned here in misery after him. During this rapid movement through time he could not see them, of course, although here and there he had the deceptive feeling that there was someone else with him. During the instants of darkness that were nights, a shape seemed to bulge on the bed across from him, but this illusion was too brief to make anything of it. In the flashes of lightning that were days, something would flicker in front of him periodically, a certain hint of movement, but it was as cryptic as a flash seen out of the corner of the eye.

The ceiling disappeared so suddenly that he did not have time to catch his breath. It was there one moment and then suddenly gone without a trace, as though a giant had taken a huge lid off the monastery. At the same time, all the partition walls were removed, leaving only the solid outer walls that no longer had any windows.

The rapidly changing days and nights were incomparably more exciting with the entire firmament spread over his head than before, when he had only had a tiny corner of the sky. The entire universe seemed to be hurriedly whispering some secret message to him. . . .

But he was not given the time to figure it out. Just as mysteriously as the lid was lost, it returned a few moments later, although not the old one. He found himself inside an enormous closed space over which there rose a gigantic dome. Only cathedrals boast such roofs, he thought, but this certainly was not a cathedral; their domes did not have a wide slit cut through the center, let alone a large cylinder pointing upward through that opening.

He did not realize that the voyage was over because there was no slowing down; it happened all at once. He was looking at the empty opening in the vault over his head, but many heartbeats had to pass before he finally noticed that the alternating light and darkness had stopped. The night sky that settled in his eyes was sprinkled with the clusters of stars found in the thin air of mountain peaks.

A click in his hand jolted him out of the paralysis that had overcome him. The watch had completely slipped his mind, although it had been in his outstretched palm the entire time. Now it had closed, since its magic work was finished. He first thought to put it in his pocket but then decided he should keep it in his hand; his first idea would have shown inadmissible disrespect.

He slowly and timidly began to turn around in the semidarkness of the large area. As wondrous things whose purpose he could not divine entered his field of vision, he remembered the tempter's words; he had said that in the end he would have seen for himself that it was an astronomical observatory.

The tempter must have greatly overestimated him. There was nothing here he could recognize: no telescope, sextant, map of the stars, or brass model of the planetary system.

Instead, the circular wall was covered for the most part with unusual windows. They shone in a variety of colors, but it could not have been the light from outside because it was dark. Some forms were moving on them, and he cautiously went up to one part of the wall to get a better look. They turned out to be yellow numbers that proceeded as far as the eye could see in horizontal rows against blue or red backgrounds, appearing at one end and disappearing at the other, although the device that was writing them was nowhere to be seen.

He would have stood there a long time staring at this sparkling display, whose meaning he had not even tried to penetrate, had it not been for the sound of quiet voices he suddenly heard behind him. He started in complete surprise. During his first moment of confusion, all he felt was the instinctive need to hide somewhere, but there was no time for that. When he turned around, just a few steps from him were two tall figures—a man and a woman—dressed in long white robes, heading his way, talking in hushed tones.

They had to see him; it was unavoidable, since he was standing right there in front of them, paralyzed and bewildered. But they passed right by him, paying no attention to his conspicuous presence, as though he were completely invisible. He stood there for a long time, immobile, trying to get used to this impossibility, as his temples pounded fiercely.

The figures in white went up to one of the windows that was considerably larger than the others and was unlit and started to touch some of the bumps that protruded under it. The window suddenly lit up, but it did not have the stream of numbers as on the others. It showed something that the prisoner could finally make sense of. The star field seemed far denser, brighter, and sharper but basically did not differ from what he had seen through his small telescope.

But how could the picture in the window and the telescope be the same? What kind of window was that? The answer soon followed, but his readiness to believe took considerably more time. The two people continued to touch the bumps, and the scene slowly started to change. The change itself was clear to him, but he could not figure out how it was done. He would have achieved the same effect if he were to slowly raise his telescope: some stars would disappear under the lower edge, while others would appear above. But here the window did not move at all.

Then he heard something buzzing behind him. It was quite feeble, like the sound of a distant bee. He probably would not have turned around if he hadn't been compelled by the pins and needles at the back of his head—the tension of premonition. Something was going on behind his back, something big was moving.

The heavy, upright cylinder in the lower part of the slit in the dome slowly rose toward the highest point, although he could not see how it moved. It seemed to be doing so by itself, without the help of ropes and a winch.

He caught on to what was going on before the cylinder stopped at an angle of about seventy degrees. So, the tempter had not overestimated him too much. In any case, it was only a matter of proportions here. Even though it was gigantic, the telescope had kept its original shape. What he could not understand was that the eyepiece had been moved. Instead of being the only place it could be, at the bottom of the cylinder, it was on the wall like a big window that everyone could look at.

The picture on it stabilized just for a moment, and then a new change started. The stars began to flow over all the edges as though the telescope were rushing through the air at an unbelievable speed, although it was resting immobile. It penetrated more and more into the dark expanse, reaching for unattainable infinity.

The impression was intoxicating, delightful. And then, as if this were not enough, music echoed. The woman in white went for a moment to a smaller window and touched something. At the same moment, the crystal sounds of heavenly harmony reverberated from all sides. He could not see any musicians or instruments, he could not understand a thing, but he did not care. He was experiencing what one experiences perhaps once in a lifetime: ascension.

The two climaxes merged into one. One point in the middle of the picture started to get bigger, to expand. At first it was a star like the countless ones around it, then it was a circle, then a ring, and then finally it burst into a lacy flower that filled the entire window. The moment it opened its rosy, vaporous petals, the music streamed upward, greeting with an upsurge of joy the appearance of the yellow nucleus—the hidden eye of the Creator himself.

He was not filled with frustration when everything around him suddenly froze and became silent. He knew this would happen, that the watch cover had to open again. The moment of the about-face was perfect. The epiphany had just taken place. Dared he hope for anything greater?

Return trips always seem shorter than departures. There were no more surprises and wonders to slow down time. Even though he felt awe as he watched the reverse sequence of what he had seen before—the disappearance of the dome, the return of the barred windows, the formation of doors and beds, the flickering of days and nights—his thoughts were elsewhere.

His confused thoughts that gradually formed a crucial question.

The end of the voyage came abruptly once again, just as when he arrived in the future. At first, while his eyes were still blinded by the flashes, he could not make out anyone on the other side of the cell. Icy fingers of horror tightened around his chest. What if he wasn't there anymore? If he had only been playing with him? That would be just like the tempter. Then he never would know. . . .

"So?" came a gentle voice from the darkness.

He tried to muffle the sigh of relief, but such effort was futile in the murky silence of the night. "You said the observatory would be named after me, didn't you?" There was no time to beat around the bush; he had to get straight to the point.

"Yes."

"Why?"

"What do you mean?"

"Because of the discovery I made or because I was burned at the stake for not renouncing it?"

"For both one and the other, although considerably more for the act of sacrifice. You know, in the age you just visited, your discovery has only historical value. It has not been refuted, but it is secondary, insignificant, almost forgotten. As you have seen, things have advanced much farther. But your burning will not be forgotten."

From somewhere in the heart of the monastery came the sound of heavy footsteps. It was not just two guards. A larger group was walking through the corridors.

"Does that mean I have no choice?" asked the prisoner quickly. "If the observatory is named after me because I was burned at the stake, then it necessarily follows that there is no way I can avoid that fate. But I can still do it. I still have free will. They're coming. What if I say yes when they ask me to renounce my discovery? That would spare me from the stake but would change the future, wouldn't it? And the future cannot be changed; I saw it with my own eyes."

The steps stopped for a moment, and then in the distance echoed the harsh sound of a barred partition door being opened.

"That's right. You can't change what you saw. And you saw only what is irrefutable, what you cannot influence in any way. What you did not see, however, is whether the observatory is named after you."

The prisoner opened his mouth to say something, but nothing came out. His sight had returned in the meantime, so that now in the obscure light of dawn pouring in from the high window he could make out the contours of his visitor.

His head was somehow elongated, as though he had something tall on it.

"No, I did not deceive you, if that's what you're thinking," he continued. "The observatory really will be named after you if you are burned at the stake. But if you are not, it will be named after someone else. One of your students, for example, who will be braver than you. There is no predetermination. Your free will determines what will happen. You will choose between a horrible death in flames and the penitent life of a royal astronomer under the wing of the church, whose comfort will be disturbed only by the scorn of a handful of students and perhaps a guilty conscience: between satisfying your own conceit and the wise insight that it actually makes no difference whom the observatory is named after. I do not envy you. It is not an easy choice."

The rumbling steps stopped in front of the cell door, and a key was thrust into the large lock.

"You know what I will decide?" said the prisoner hurriedly in a soft voice. It was more a statement than a question.

"I know," answered the gentle voice.

The rusty hinges screeched sharply, and into the small cell came first a large turnkey with a torch raised high and after him two Inquisition interrogators in the purple robes of the high priesthood. The soldier who came in last was also holding a torch. There was no more room inside, so the three remaining soldiers had to wait in the corridor.

In the smoky light the prisoner squinted hard at the figure on the bed across from him. The strange object on his head was some sort of cylindrical hat with a wide brim, and its slanted shadow completely hid the man's face.

He had not expected his visitor to stay there. Would he let the others see him? But no one paid any attention to him, as though he were not there, as though he were invisible. In other circumstances this would have confused the prisoner completely, but owing to his recent experience he accepted it as quite natural.

"Lazar," said the first priest, addressing him in an official tone, "this is the last time you will be asked: do you renounce your heresy and penitently accept the teachings of our Holy Mother the Church?"

The prisoner did not take his eyes off the figure in black, but he had turned into a statue. He sat with head bowed, silent, just like an old man who had fallen asleep, with his white hands leaning on the top of his cane. He seemed indifferent, as if all this had nothing to do with him, as though he were not the least bit interested. The silence became heavy from the tenseness, the expectation.

And then, finally, the royal astronomer slowly turned toward the inquisitors and gave his monosyllabic answer.

THE PALEOLINGUIST

I

THE KNOCK ECHOED LOUDLY IN THE HOLLOW SILENCE, MAKING her start.

She had not heard the steps approaching the door to her office. She must have dozed off again. Her round, wire-rimmed reading glasses had slipped to the tip of her nose because her head was bowed, chin on her chest. The book was still open in front of her on the desk in the lamplight, but she was drowsy and could not remember its title right away. These catnaps were becoming more and more frequent, making her feel very ill at ease as a result. Not because someone might find her in that unseemly position. She was not afraid of that; almost no one visited her anymore, not even her students, let alone her colleagues. She was an embarrassment to herself.

The knock came again. Brief and somehow reserved, hesitating. Certainly not as loud as it seemed the first time. She looked around in confusion, wondering what time of day it was. The only window in her office looked onto the skylight, but this name was quite inappropriate since the narrow shaft that went through the middle of the building from the roof to the basement was filled only with gloom even on the sunniest days.

There was a simpler way to find out the time, but it would take her at least a few minutes to find her wristwatch in the multitude of large and small items that covered her desk in disorder. And she could not let the visitor wait that long, whoever he or she might be. Visitors were rare and therefore precious.

"Come in," she said. And then, since she thought she had said it too softly, she repeated in a louder voice: "Come in."

She did not recognize the person who appeared at the door. The neon lighting from the hallway illuminated him from behind, but even if the light had shone on his front, she would not have been able to discover very much without her other glasses, which were also buried somewhere on the desk. The only thing she could conclude with certainty about the hazy outline was that he was a tall man in a dark cloak.

She pondered for a moment but could think of no one she knew who fit that description. That, however, still did not mean anything. She had learned with increasing certainty during the passing years that memory was a very unreliable support, particularly where the recent past was concerned. The more distant past was considerably sharper, which was rather apropos in view of her profession. But it made no difference: everything would become clear when the visitor started to speak. She had a hard time remembering faces, but she never forgot a voice, ever. This was probably the only place where senility had kindly spared her from its humiliating veil.

"It's not easy to find you. You're completely hidden here in the basement." She had not heard this voice before. It sounded deep and drawn out, almost melodic. It would be impossible not to remember it, even without her aptitude.

"Oh, it makes no difference. When no one is looking for you, then it's all the same where you are. But are you certain that you're in the right place?"

"This is the office for paleolinguistics, isn't it?" It was more a statement than a question.

"Yes. Or rather what's left of it. In happier times we even had a brass plate that said so, but ever since we moved here, no one has taken the trouble to put it up. Maybe they're waiting for me to do it."

Continuing to stand in the doorway, the visitor looked about the gloom of the rather small room. Three walls were covered with metal shelves, and the books and journals on them were more stacked, even thrown, than placed in an orderly fashion. A narrow vitrine rising to the low ceiling with its hot water pipes was on part of the fourth wall next to the window. It was full of tiny broken statues, pieces of pottery, and the remains of simple stone implements. These objects were also displayed without any order, often one on top of another as though the vitrine were a storage cabinet. Under the window next to the desk on a wooden backless chair covered with newspapers was a hot plate with a black kettle. Several used tea bags were lying on the newspaper like tropical fish that had died of asphyxiation.

"This is exactly as I imagined it," said the man at last.

"You imagined *this?*" she asked, bewildered.

"Yes, your office. Where you work."

She squinted, trying to focus her eyes better. "Is that supposed to be a compliment or a reproach?"

"A compliment, of course. How else could it be? I am an admirer of yours."

At first she did not know how to respond. She slowly took off her reading glasses and put them on the desk. When she finally spoke, her voice was critical. "If this is some sort of joke, then I must say it is rather out of place."

"Why do you think it's a joke?"

"I do not have admirers. I have never had any."

"But your work certainly deserves them."

She got up out of her armchair, feeling numb from sitting so long, and started to rummage through the things on her desk, looking for her other glasses. She searched for several moments, and then when she couldn't find them, she waved her hand in angry dismissal, turned her blurry eyes toward the door, and said in a voice that was more nervous than she intended, "Oh, come in, for heaven's sake. We can't talk while you're in the hallway."

He entered, closed the door after him, and then stopped, uncertain where he should sit. There was another armchair in front of the desk, but it had a load of tattered folders on it with a fairly large stone figure on the top; with considerable help of the imagination, it looked like a bulging female torso.

"Put that somewhere, on the floor, it makes no difference," she said, noticing that he did not know what to do.

He did it with utmost caution, as though holding some sort of relic in his hands. When he sat down, the springs on the armchair squeaked in complaint.

Now he was closer to her and partially illuminated by the light from her table lamp, so that even without her other glasses she could make out certain details that she had not noticed before. In his lap he laid his derby, his cane with its decorated top, and a pair of white gloves. She had never given much thought to how she dressed and did not pay attention to what other people wore, but she found this quite amazing. It was as though he had come out of a play set in olden times, she thought, smiling to herself.

The man just sat there without a word and looked at her. She soon began to fidget under his inquisitive stare. Unconsciously she started to fix her disheveled strands of gray hair as she thought over what to say to the stranger. Why had she asked him to come in? Admirer! As if she were so credulous or vain.

"So, you are interested in paleolinguistics?"

"Yes, very much so."

"Why?"

He did not answer right away. He started to slowly draw his fingers along the smooth edge of the derby in his hand. "An unusual question from someone who has devoted her entire life to that field," he said at last.

"Not at all unusual," she replied. "The very fact that I squandered my whole life in paleolinguistics gives me the clear-cut right to ask you that."

"Do you think you squandered your life?"

She stared at his blurry face outside the lamplight. She could not guess his age. His voice was not a reliable indicator. Judging by it alone, the man could have been in his twenties or even his forties. For his sake, she hoped it was the former; it would be much easier for him to lose his illusions. If only she had been lucky enough to have had some sense knocked into her at that age.

"Take a good look around you again. You are in a tiny basement room that was the janitor's storage before and will return to that function when I retire in several months. Since I am not able to take these things with me, the books and other artifacts will all be thrown away. Useless. And even if I took them, it would not make much difference. Everything would end up on the garbage heap after my death. There, that is the best measure of the success of a life devoted to paleolinguistics. So please listen to my advice: get interested in something else. Anything. Forget primeval language and the far-off past. Who is interested in that in the modern world? Don't ruin your future without reason."

"The past and the future, yes," replied the visitor, lost in thought. He paused for a moment, and she thought a smile flickered on his face. But she could not be sure. "I think that there are other measures that can be used to evaluate what you have achieved." He said it with determination, like a man who knows what he is talking about.

She looked at him inquisitively. "What, for example?"

"If it weren't for you, the department of paleolinguistics would never have been founded."

"Probably, but what has been the benefit of that? Do you know the largest number of new students I have had all these years?"

He clearly did not understand this as a question and so did not reply. He did not even shrug his shoulders.

"Eight. And that was long ago; it's been almost a quarter of a century. The average has been three and a half students. And only two of them at most finish their studies. Sometimes not even one. But not because I was too strict. On the contrary, I was considered a very"—she stopped for a moment, looking for the right word—"helpful examiner, which gave me a bad reputation among my colleagues. The young people simply gave up, primarily because they were disappointed, even though I did all I could to stimulate their interest not only in the technical aspects of the origin of language but also in a considerably less tedious subject: early human communities. They are inseparable, in any case. But nothing seemed to work. I never understood what they actually expected when they decided to major in paleolinguistics. No one made them choose it."

"You cannot blame yourself for the students' poor response. You said yourself that we live in a time that is not particularly predisposed toward the past."

She squinted at him briefly and then continued to follow her line of thinking, paying no attention to his comforting words.

"In the last four years, no one signed up in my department. How can you keep your position as lecturer if you have no one to lecture to? Only if the administration is lenient toward you. They didn't have to do it. They probably wouldn't have if it weren't for my age. I stayed here just because the dean was considerate enough to support me, although it would have been natural to fire me. He knew that at my age I have nowhere to go. I knew that myself, so I swallowed my pride and let them put me in this cubbyhole. Don't look a gift horse in the mouth, particularly not when the gift is given out of pity. What else could I have done, anyway?"

She stopped talking, wondering why she was telling all this to a stranger. She was only putting them both in an awkward situation. But the matter concerned him, too. He had come there with an idealized notion about paleolinguistics, hadn't he? Would it be fair to let him go without seeing its other side? Certainly not. In any case, she had not had the opportunity to talk to someone for a long time, to pour out her grief. There were no more students, and her colleagues avoided her more or less openly.

"Now I'm on sabbatical. That was the last chance for me to reach retirement age in this position. I was given a leave of absence quite easily. It was actually a gift. I didn't even have to present any sort of research plan, as is customary. No project that I would work on. No one even asked. No one expects anything from me anymore."

"But you have done so much already. You wrote several fundamental works on paleolinguistics. Isn't that more than enough?"

Her blurry eyes started to wander over the multitude of objects covering the desk in front of her. Had she known she would have a visitor, she would have tidied up the office a bit. Actually, she had been reproaching herself for some time for the clutter surrounding her, but she could never make up her mind to do anything about it. There was no incentive. What was the purpose, since she would be leaving there in a few months? But then, couldn't that be expanded to all of life itself? Why make any effort at all when everything was transient? She used to know the answer, it had seemed obvious and irrefutable, but with the passage of time it had become hazier and darker.

"Would you like some tea?"

He did not answer right away. He seemed to hesitate. "No, thank you," he said at last.

It was only then that she realized there was just one teacup. Had the man accepted her offer, she would have had to do without tea, something that would not have been easy for her. She had become a real addict. Several years ago, when the doctor had advised her to stop drinking coffee because of high blood pressure, she had switched to tea, primarily to appease her habit of constantly sipping something hot. When she reached seven cups a day, she realized she had gone too far, but it was too late by then.

"I would. Do you mind?"

"Not at all."

She hobbled over to the small, cracked ceramic sink that stood next to the window, picking up the kettle on her way. Although her vision was very poor without her glasses, she did not need them to make tea. She had gone through this sequence of simple motions so many times that she could have managed in total darkness.

"There is nothing truly fundamental in my works," she said in a hushed voice, after plugging in the hot plate and returning to her armchair. "It is all just an educated guess, at best."

For a few moments all that was heard was the sound of water leaking in thin streams from several spots on the cracked exterior of the kettle, evaporating when they hit the red-hot plate.

"What do you mean?" asked the visitor at length.

"Do you know the first thing I told my students so they knew right from the start what they were involved in? Paleolinguistics is not an exact science. It cannot be, since, in the strictest sense of that term, the subject of study is missing. Primeval language has been dead for a very long time. We have no direct evidence of it. And even the indirect evidence is quite scanty. All we do is make more or less questionable reconstructions. We try to recompose a mosaic whose original appearance is unknown, and we are not even certain that we are using the right stones."

"But didn't you convincingly show that living languages and the dead ones that have been preserved both contain traces of primeval language? Which is natural, in any case. They all arose from it, didn't they?"

"Convincingly, yes. Perhaps. There is one person, however, whom I have never managed to completely convince of this. The only one I really care about."

"Who is that?"

"Myself, of course."

The kettle suddenly whistled. She got up slowly, unplugged the hot plate, took a small tea bag out of a half-empty yellow box on the desk, lifted the kettle's little lid, quickly removed her hand so the steam would not burn her, waited for the cloud rushing out to disperse, and dropped the tea bag into the boiling water.

"They say you shouldn't put the tea bag in right away. If the water is too hot, it kills the aroma of the tea. But I don't have the patience to wait."

"You are unfair to yourself. You must not doubt your whole life's work. Just think of the enormous effort you have made."

"What else can I do? Resort to self-delusion? Repeat to myself that it can't be all in vain since I made such a tremendous effort? But effort itself is by no means a guarantee of success. There is something, however, that is even worse than doubt. The hardest thing for me is that the doubt can never be removed: there is no way to know how close I came to primeval language. But there's no one to blame for that. I knew from the beginning that was the main anathema of the field I had chosen."

"Except if you were to go back into the past."

She smiled at him briefly. "Yes, except if I were to go back into the past. I know many people who would sell their soul to the devil without the slightest hesitation for such an opportunity. All kinds of historians. People like me, obsessed with long-ago times. But either the soul is not enough payment or the devil himself is not that powerful. Probably the latter. Unfortunately, there's no going back into the past."

"If there were, would you accept the devil's offer?"

She looked at him without speaking for a time and then got up to wash out her cup and pour the tea. When she returned to the desk, the newspaper that covered the chair with the hot plate had a new fish steaming in agony.

"I don't think the devil would choose me. What use would he have for such a poor, worn-out soul as mine?"

"Maybe he wouldn't even ask for your soul."

"Oh, don't be naive. The devil isn't generous. You don't get something for nothing from him."

"I agree. He always collects payment for his services. But there are other rewards in addition to the soul that he might find more attractive."

"What else could he expect from me in return?"

"The devil is a sadist above all. He enjoys people's suffering. If he helped you return to the past, he would be putting you in twofold torment."

She greedily took a sip of tea. She knew it was still hot, that it would burn the sensitive inside of her mouth, but the addict in her had run out of patience again. Conversation with this stranger had become rather pointless, even though he amused her in some odd way.

"Twofold?" she repeated inquiringly.

"Yes. Imagine that you go back in time and there, on the spot, you reliably establish how things were. What would you do with that knowledge?"

"Well, I don't know. Publish it, probably."

"But you are a scientist. Wouldn't you ruin your credibility by citing that your knowledge stems from a trip into the past arranged by the devil? They would proclaim you a charlatan at best. At worst you'd end up in an insane asylum."

Before she replied, she took another long sip of hot tea. The cup was already half empty.

"Then I wouldn't publish it. But the devil still would have no reason to rejoice. I told you that I only care about convincing one person. And for her sake it would not be necessary to publish anything. She would be convinced without it, by firsthand experience." She stopped a moment, smiling again. "Let me hear what other trap the devil has prepared for me."

"What is the fundamental hypothesis of your field, that is, all fields that study the past?" The visitor had not acquired her facetious tone. His voice was as serious as before, and she thought it was quite pleasant. Dignified. Too bad she had not found her glasses. A man with such a voice simply had to have an agreeable face.

"The immutability of what has happened, if that is what you had in mind."

"That's right, the past cannot be changed. That fact would be jeopardized, however, if someone from the future appeared in the past. The devil's services would desecrate something that is older and must remain inviolable. What would be the use of learning firsthand about the past if it were no longer final?"

"Why do you think that a visitor from the future would destroy the past? If he were a scientist—and we're talking about that kind of time traveler, aren't we?—it would not be in his interest. On the contrary, he would have every reason to remain an inconspicuous observer."

"Yes, he would have every reason. But would that be enough? There would be enormous temptation to influence the course of events. Take, for example, a historian who goes back to some turning point in history. If he remains simply an observer, events will take their well-known course that will result in the death of a large number of innocent people. On the other hand, it could all be avoided by his involvement. In this case, what would prevail inside him: the dispassionate scientist or the man who realizes that if he does not take any measures, his conscience will be burdened with unbearable guilt? It would not be an easy choice, and this would give the devil great pleasure."

She stared for a moment at the bottom of the empty cup in front of her before answering.

"Not every traveler to the past would necessarily come up against such a difficult choice. There are peaceful times, without turning points. For example, if I went back to the period I studied, I could be an impartial observer without any encumbrance because nothing would drive me to get involved in the course of events, to change the future. Historically speaking, it was a completely innocent age. I'm afraid the devil would not get his due."

"There is no innocent age." He said it softer than before, as though it were confidential, secret. "Have you heard of the butterfly effect?"

She had heard of it but could by no means remember what it was. Even if her memory had been in better shape, it would quite likely have slipped her mind. She had never fancied such innovations. Her science was classical, more elementary. To avoid answering, she got up to pour a new cup of tea, and he waited for her to return to the desk.

"A butterfly suddenly starts to fly, urged by who knows what, highly unaware of the fact that this movement might start a chain of events whose far-off final link is a storm of continental proportions on the other side of the world. The flutter of tiny wings sets the chaos equation in motion, whose solution can be completely disproportionate to this infinitesimal movement. A tiny cause sometimes leads to enormous effects."

"Yes, I know about that," she replied, "only I don't see what that has to do with what we were talking about."

"Regardless of how firmly you are resolved not to change the past, what happens does not depend on you alone. Quite unintentionally, by your very presence, you might bring about the butterfly effect. Maybe even literally. Imagine that your sudden appearance there disturbs a butterfly that has been idly perched on a flower. Frightened, it suddenly takes flight, and several days later, far from there, someone dies in a storm who was not supposed to die at all, someone who is the starting point of an inverse pyramid of history. You might be convinced that this outcome is highly unlikely, but the devil, as an experienced gambler, would not hold back from accepting the wager. It would actually be a safe bet. Chaos is his kingdom, when it comes right down to it."

"But if this is how things stand, if the devil can't lose, what's stopping him from coming with his offer? He hasn't visited me, or anyone else in my field as far as I know. And among us he would find the most prominent victims."

She expected an answer from the other side of the desk, but there was none forthcoming. As the silence in the gloomy basement room deepened, distant unintelligible sounds from the upper levels could be heard.

"So, we are back to where we started," she said, finally breaking the silence. "Going into the past is clearly not within the devil's power."

"Maybe it is," said the melodic voice in return, "but of the kind that would not give him the reward he wants if he were to offer it to someone. That is why there is no offer."

Now it was her turn to remain silent. She peered in bewilderment at the foggy figure across from her.

"If there were neither the temptation nor the opportunity to change the past, then the returnee would feel no torment that would suffice the devil as payment."

"But is that possible? Doesn't it follow from your story about the butterfly that the very act of stepping into the past would inevitably change it?"

"Yes, it does follow, but only if one went physically into the past. And it does not have to be that way."

She raised her cup to her lips, but the tea was already lukewarm. This was not the way she liked it; it was tasteless. She found a bit of empty space on the desk and put the cup there.

"Then how would it be?"

"What do you do when you watch a documentary film?" said the visitor, answering her question with one of his own. "You go into the past without the opportunity of changing anything. Film editors do have a few tricks at their disposal, but that doesn't count: that would be falsifying the past and not truly changing it. The viewer of a documentary film is in the position of the ideal unbiased observer: he can in no way influence the past."

"Yes, but that is only true for more recent history. It is really possible to return to the past that way. At least partially. The filmed version enchants us with its images and sound, but reality is something richer. But let's put that aside. I must remind you that, unfortunately, no documentary films have been made about the age that interests me."

If he noticed the irony in her voice, it was not revealed by any change in his tone. "Of course not. I was not even thinking of such a return to the past. It is, as you say, quite incomplete. But the comparison with films is rather convenient. Imagine such a film about the past that would act upon all your senses, not just sight and hearing. A film in which you would feel exactly the same way you do in reality, except that you could not take part in it, change it. You would have the role of an infinitely empowered viewer who sees, hears, and feels everything, yet remains invisible and inaudible, unobserved."

She blinked. "That sounds like a ghost to me."

The visitor gave a brief laugh, resonant and clear. "Yes, the viewer would be like a ghost, for all practical purposes."

"That's all fine, but there are no such films about the past. None have been made."

She thought there would be some comment from the dusty armchair, but silence greeted her once again. She closed her eyes for a moment and rubbed the bridge of her nose with thumb and forefinger, thinking that it was time to bring the conversation to a close. What else was there to say? They had reached the topic of ghosts, hadn't they? Even though she was happy that someone had visited her, now she was feeling tired. A person should not be overly indulgent toward admirers.

"I wonder what time it is. My watch is lost somewhere in this mess on the desk. I can't wear it on my wrist all the time—it rubs—and then I can never remember where I put it."

She assumed that he would look at his left wrist, but he reached under his cloak and took out a pocket watch. A dull golden reflection danced about it, and she thought how strange it was. She could not remember the last time she had seen a watch like that. Had they come back into fashion? She knew nothing about fashion, but then how could she since she never went anywhere, never saw anyone, spending the entire day between these four basement walls.

He handed her the watch. She took it impassively, simply because he had offered it. It was only when she had it in her hand that she wondered why he had not simply told her the time instead of letting her find out for herself.

She brought the object right up close to her eyes, so she could see without her glasses, but did not open the lid right away because her attention was attracted to the engraving on its bulging surface. A capital letter *E* was ornate, with a series of decorative loops at the ends, just like initials from some old-fashioned manuscript. Quite unusual, is what flashed through her mind. *E* as in Eva. Like it was meant for me.

And then she moved the little catch and the lid jumped up.

II

There were no hands. There was no face. Just a bright circle that contained some kind of image. The image was not quite steady but trembled as though alive. Confused, she brought the watch a little closer to get a better look, but when she wanted to stop it, it kept coming closer all by itself, without her influence. The casing started to get bigger, like a round fissure in reality that quickly expanded before her, its brilliance crowding out the gloom of the basement room, until it had pushed it all the way over the edge of the world.

She was blinded at first. Her pupils were accustomed to the poor light in the office and needed some time to adjust to the bright midday sun. But the rest of her senses immediately began to absorb the rich impressions of her new surroundings. She was struck by the unknown smells of wild vegetation, dense and abundant, prickling her and stinging her nostrils as though someone had thrown a handful of pollen into her face. Her ears were filled with the undulating sound of tall, brittle blades of grass and the buzzing and humming of a multitude of insects engrossed in their ritual dances. The breeze reached her skin in uneven gusts, stroking her face and hands with the softest touch.

She knew what she would see even before her eyesight returned, but there was still no lack of surprise. She was in the middle of a field that stretched all around in gentle folds as far as the eye could see, but what her senses of smell, hearing, and touch could not tell her was that countless butterflies covered the expanse around her like some flickering, brightly colored rug. They were flying low over the ground cover or resting on it, completely devoted to their harmless business which, as she had recently learned, could result in unforeseeable disaster.

She froze at that thought. What if her appearance upset them? What if they suddenly started to fly, thereby disturbing something that should not be disturbed? She stopped breathing when a butterfly left a purple flower with large petals and zigzagged toward her, lazily fluttering its spotted wings. When it got near her face, she instinctively closed her eyes, helplessly expecting it to fly into her at any moment. But no crash occurred. When she opened her eyes, the butterfly was gone. She first thought that it must have turned at the last instant. The other possibility was so unbelievable that she simply refused to accept it.

But soon afterward, when a somewhat stronger gust of wind raised an excited cloud of butterflies, she nonetheless had to accept the impossible. They flew through her as though she were not there, as though she were made of some airy substance, transparent, nonexistent, unreal.

At first she just stood there without moving, completely confused, and watched the cloud stream through her body. She felt this rising tide like a weak sting, like light goose pimples flowing on the surface of her skin. The cloud had already thinned out when she finally came out of her paralysis and extended her hand toward the last butterflies. She could touch them in flight. The touch was irrefutable, although one-sided: the tiny wings yielded unfeelingly to her invisible fingers in their multicolored fluttering.

She remained undecided for a time after the last butterfly had gone. Serious, distressing questions were welling up from part of her consciousness, but she quickly smothered the tiresome voice that only spoiled the magic. What difference did it make that it was impossible when it seemed so dreamy, so intoxicating?

She had no reason to go in any particular direction, so she simply went straight ahead. She did so unconsciously, taking a step forward, but instead of her foot landing on the grass again, as it should have, it continued in the air.

She did not realize right away that she was flying. At first she thought she'd lost her balance and would fall, but she never did. She stayed in midair, without support, bewildered because she had always been afraid of heights, although she was barely at knee level. She wished in panic to go down, and the very next moment she was resting on the ground again.

Some time passed before she mustered the courage to move again. She thought she must look like a child awkwardly trying to take its first steps. This time there was no need to step forward. All she had to do was will it: she wanted to fly—and the same instant she was again in the air, infinitely light, incorporeal.

She first took a horizontal birdlike position, extending her arms like wings, but quickly realized that this was not necessary. Undignified, actually. Owing to her years, it was much more becoming for her to be in the air as she was on the ground, so she straightened up with her arms crossed on her chest, as though standing on an invisible pedestal.

Fear faded and gave way to fascination. The experience of unhindered flight was thrilling, giddy. First she streamed high up until she reached the fluffy substance of a small cloud, and then, barely resisting the urge to scream with excitement, she started back down, enjoying the sight of the green carpet approaching at lightning-quick speed. She stopped right above it effortlessly, without disturbing the swarm of buzzing insects quarreling over a cluster of yellow and red flowers.

When she soared to the bottom of the heavens again, she caught sight of something she had missed her first time up there. Her surprise was actually twofold, and she suddenly stopped in the middle of nothingness. When she saw a thin column of smoke rising on the distant horizon, it flashed through her mind that this should not be possible: she did not have her glasses with her. They had been left behind in the office, somewhere in the disorder on her desk. But it seemed that in this new form they were not necessary; she could see the spiraling sign of someone's fire quite clearly without them.

She hurried in that direction like an eagle that has spotted its prey, driven by impatience and foreboding. The suppressed questions started to surge to the surface again. If she was truly where she suspected, although all this was beyond reason, of course, then she had found her destination.

The tribe was small—she counted only twelve members. Next to the fire were two old women, an old man, and four children of different ages. The other five adults—how stunted they were!—were dispersed in a broad circle around this temporary habitat. They were engaged in what people of that early age spent most of their time doing: painstakingly collecting food—different berries, roots, shriveled fruit, small rodents.

She did not descend next to the fire, but a bit farther away. She could feel her heart thudding in her immaterial chest. The voices of the old people and children were muffled and indistinct, but that is what she wanted. She was not yet ready. When she was, she would go among them—a ghost who would know as soon as she heard their first words whether her former life had any meaning or not.

She wondered what price she would have to pay for this unique privilege. It certainly could not be the assurance that she would not return from here. Even if she had that impossible watch, what was there to go back to? Lonely drudgery in a dark basement cubbyhole? The humiliation brought by neglect and old age? The unremovable doubts that would maliciously follow her to the end? No, staying here would be a reward and not a punishment. So what would it be?

The answer came with the wind. The current of air brought to her insensate nostrils the hot smell of steam from the sooty earthen vessel in which water was boiling over the fire. The old women were cleaning some dried herbs, getting them ready for the pot, chatting idly, just as would be done in the countless centuries to follow.

Tea, of course!

An inaudible scream was wrenched from the addict. She felt neither hunger nor thirst, which would be quite natural in this state. But the longing for a hot cup of tea that suddenly inundated her was something much more than a physical need. The delusive impression that the familiar tonic was flowing through the inside of her mouth, the promise that her overpowering need would soon be satisfied, had the same effect as real pain.

As she was filled with despair, she thought that she would not have accepted had she known the price she would have to pay. But she had not actually been given the choice. All right, then, she concluded after getting hold of herself, there's no turning back. The price has been paid, even though unwillingly. All that was left was to take what was hers in return.

And she headed for the fire to meet the voices of the primeval language that would tell her the simple truth.

■ □ ■ □ ■

THE WATCHMAKER

I

THE CLOCKS STRUCK 6:00 P.M. SIMULTANEOUSLY, JUST AS THEY should in a reputable watchmaker's shop. The old man's trained ears had been carefully monitoring this sound, and they could not detect any divergence: not a single one of the four clocks adorning the walls of the rather small, ground-floor premises was either early or late. This was the only harmony that linked them, however, for what followed afterward was total discordance.

The grandfather clock, with its pendulum in a casing of worn mahogany and door of thick, etched glass, grumbled in a deep, solemn bass, like a mustachioed sergeant grenadier giving orders at a parade. The brass dwarf hit his worn hammer on the hanging bronze rod, creating a clear, sharp sound resembling the echo of distant bells. The call of the wooden cuckoo rushing out the round opening of the gaily colored alpine house had lost its original rapture long ago, becoming harsh and piercing. Finally, the chipped ceramic pair of dancers in ballroom attire nimbly started to turn on the small circular podium at the first bars of an old-fashioned waltz.

Although they started simultaneously, the sounds that struck the hour did not end at the same time. First the cuckoo went silent, suddenly, like a death rattle; it seemed almost as if someone with delicate nerves or no ear for its tired singing had ungraciously wrung its neck. The waltz and the ringing lasted about the same time, competing to the final note for futile advantage. The drawn-out tones of the grandfather clock filled the shop the longest, its very size making it natural for the clock to have the last word.

When the final grumble of the grenadier's bass had died out, the old man reached adroitly for a small pocket on the left side of his vest. He took out a gold-plated pocket watch with a thick chain, raised the lid—which had TO J. FROM M. engraved on the inside in large, ornate letters—and briefly nodded, satisfied that it was truly six o'clock. This was not an expression of distrust toward the other clocks which had just informed him of the same fact quite loudly and precisely. For more than a quarter of a century he had been carrying out this ritual every evening before he closed the shop and went home, as a sign of respect for a special memory. And a pain.

But he was not fated to spend that evening in the usual way: closing the door to the shop, taking the short walk along the most often empty street to the small, excessively neat attic apartment where no one waited for him, preparing a simple and for the most part tasteless meal that would probably satisfy only a bachelor or a single person, and going to bed. Sleep would rarely bring him refreshment or oblivion; it mainly gave him restless dreams that returned him to the past. He could not leave the past, not even in his dreams.

He had just put the heavy watch back into his vest pocket and was about to pull the short little chain with a silver ring at the end to turn off the lamp with the green shade on his workbench behind the counter when the door opened suddenly, jangling the cluster of bells hanging above. Although mild compared to the discordant choir of the wall clocks, the unexpected sound of these signal bells made him start. He rarely had customers in his shop this late.

He looked up, but all he could make out in the gloom was the silhouette of a tall man against the dull glow of the streetlight. The man was wearing a hat, probably a derby, and a rather long cloak, and in his right hand was a cane. He stopped next to the door without going up to the counter, as though hesitating for some reason.

The old man pushed his round, metal-framed work glasses halfway down his nose and asked, trying to sound obliging, "May I help you, sir?"

The man did not reply at once. He looked around the shop as though wanting to make sure that only the two of them were there. His eyes rested a bit longer on the grandfather clock; half of the pendulum's path was in shadow, and the circular ending flickered in the other half as it reflected the muted light from outside.

The late visitor finally put his cane under his arm and took resolute steps toward the counter, at the same time taking something out of an inside pocket. When he reached him, the old man saw that he was wearing white leather gloves; he had long, slender fingers like a piano player's. His right fist was closed, and he put it palm up on the counter that was covered tightly with felt. Illuminated by the edge of light from his work lamp, its whiteness looked unnaturally bright compared to the green background and the darkness around them. The watchmaker suddenly had the impression that the man before him was a magician who was about to pull a sleight of hand.

The trick, however, did not occur, for when his hand opened, it contained quite an exemplary object: a pocket watch. The old man returned his glasses to the bridge of his nose and leaned over to have a better look. Up until then, he had been convinced that all he needed was one look at a watch in order to recognize not only the brand but also the type and even the year it was made. He had spent almost four decades working exclusively with watches. He knew them inside out, one might say. Particularly pocket watches; he was a real expert where they were concerned. He knew each little spring, gear, screw, and nut. Every little hand and face.

But here he had a surprise in store. One look was not enough. He certainly had never seen this type before. The old man knit his brow in disbelief and leaned a bit closer. He was filled with the powerful urge to take the watch from the white palm, to finger it, open it, but decency stopped him from doing so. He continued to look at it, putting his eager hands behind his back. He strove hard to find some detail he could recognize, but all his trained eye could ascertain was that the watch was exquisitely made. There was no doubt about that: it was the creation of a true master of his trade—an expert he had never heard of.

Shaking his head briefly, he straightened up and looked at the visitor inquiringly. The man's face was still in the darkness under the hat brim, so the watchmaker could not see anything. Suddenly he felt a mild prickling sensation at the base of his neck, the bristling of sparse white hairs. There was something unreal in the tall figure in front of him, something that filled him with unease, agitation.

This impression did not pass when the visitor finally spoke.

"I would like you to have a look at this watch," he said in a hoarse, dignified voice which did not need to be raised even when giving an order. A foreigner, concluded the watchmaker. Although he made an effort to say the words properly, his accent gave him away as well as a certain drawl, although not one common in travelers from the north who were the most frequent strangers in this area. It was impossible to say where he was from.

"Certainly, sir, certainly," he replied. "What is your complaint, sir? I mean, what is wrong with your watch? It is obviously quite expensive, although . . ." He opened his mouth to admit that he had never seen one like it before, but he held back at the last moment, fearing this might stop the visitor from leaving his watch with him. He certainly had to have the chance to examine it in greater detail.

"I have no complaints," said the stranger, interrupting him. "The watch is fine. But all the same, I think it would be a good idea for you to have a look at it."

"Most certainly, sir. You are quite right. A bit of precaution would certainly do no harm. On the contrary, never enough caution. You were very wise to bring your watch to be looked at. Even the best watches need regular maintenance. People do not bear that in mind, actually, they are negligent for the most part, not only toward objects, unfortunately; many misfortunes would be avoided if precautionary measures were taken...."

"There are no precautions that can thwart chance." The man said this in an even voice, as though saying something obvious, even banal. The watchmaker squinted toward the invisible face; although the statement sounded generalized, in principle, there was something in the stranger's tone that gave it the weight and credibility of personal experience.

"Yes, indeed. Of course. You understand things perfectly, sir. Chance, yes. Something you cannot influence regardless of how hard you try. For a watchmaker that is the effect of dust. I have yet to see a watch without dust, and countless numbers have gone through my hands in my many years of work. You can protect a watch however you want, even close it hermetically, but nothing helps. Dust will find a way inside, and one particle is enough—one single, solitary particle—to jeopardize the fine mechanism. You have no idea, sir, what a nightmare dust is for watchmakers."

"Yes, a particle of dust," repeated the visitor, drawing out his words, lost in thought. "The flutter of butterfly wings . . ."

The old man's eyes became suspicious. What was that supposed to mean? What "flutter"? Maybe he had wanted to say something else but expressed himself awkwardly in a foreign language—although he seemed to speak it well, at least fluently and correctly, if not without an accent. Or maybe he was some kind of crank, an eccentric? The old man was not prejudiced against foreigners and considered the stories that could be heard about their peculiarities, even abnormalities, to be exaggerated for the most part. But you never knew. There were quacks everywhere, in any case. Not even this area had been spared from them.

He had the impression that some sort of reply was expected from him but did not know what to say. Really, "butterfly wings" . . . what could he say about them that would be nice, polite? He was saved from the awkward situation by a carriage that suddenly passed by in the street. The rapid thud of horse hooves caused the plated wheels to produce a sharp rattle as they rolled over the cobblestone street. The visitor seemed to flinch a bit at this noise, turning toward the entrance. But the carriage passed in a flash, and the fading echo of its passage was quickly absorbed by the heavy silence of the evening.

"Yes," said the watchmaker when the stranger turned his unseen face toward him again, "you are completely right. There is no way to fight against chance."

"Oh, that's not what I said. I only said that you cannot thwart it, prevent it. But that does not mean that you cannot fight against it."

The old man involuntarily swallowed the lump in his throat. "Please forgive me, sir, but I'm afraid that I don't understand you very well," he replied timidly.

Before he answered, the visitor finally put the pocket watch on the felt-covered counter, as though for some reason he had concluded just that instant that he could safely let the watchmaker take his valuable timepiece. When the white glove withdrew from the lamplight, the old man had the impression that a bright trace remained after it for a few moments. With his free hand, the foreigner skillfully took the cane from under his arm and, turning slowly on his heel, pointed it at the clocks on the four walls.

"It is all a matter of time, you see," he said at last, after making a full circle and returning to face the watchmaker. His voice took on that flat quality again that spoke of reliable knowledge, his own experience.

The old man just nodded, without a word, as though this statement explained everything. One had to be careful with eccentrics; it was not advisable to contradict them.

"What makes chance so powerful? The fact that you can't foresee it. If you knew exactly which particle of dust would ruin the watch mechanism, you could remove it in time. But you can't know that until the malfunction occurs, of course."

"Of course," repeated the watchmaker like an echo, with another nod.

"Cause and effect," continued the visitor. "The particle only becomes a cause when the effect takes place—the malfunction. Never beforehand. That is why alleged clairvoyants and similar illusionary sleights of hand have no meaning. The future cannot be foretold because then one would be able to change it. And if you changed it, then it would no longer be the predicted future. You cannot prophesy: this particle is the cause of the future malfunction—and then remove it, because then there would be no malfunction, and your prophecy would have no value, either. No, the consequences must happen in any case. And they do take place. You yourself said that you have never seen a watch without dust inside. And you undertook detailed precautionary measures, everything that was within your power, to prevent it."

"Oh, I did, I did, most assuredly. You can be certain of that, sir. I hope I am not being immodest when I say that this watch repair shop has an excellent reputation for industriousness. You will see this for yourself, sir, I hope. We leave nothing to chance here. . . ."

The old man stopped, biting his tongue; it was only after he had said this last sentence that he realized the expression he used might sound inappropriate, owing to the topic of their discussion. But since the visitor did not react, he quickly continued.

"But, if you will forgive me my poor perception, sir, I cannot see how it is possible to fight against chance—your very words, sir—if the effects, the consequences, must take place?"

The foreigner did not answer at once. Led by some obscure impulse, he threw his cane a short distance into the air, then as it fell caught it adeptly near the upper end with his thumb and forefinger and started to swing the lower part as if it were a pendulum. It was only then that the old man in the gentle, milky gleam that the top of the cane was the stylized figure of an hourglass. Most likely made of ivory, he concluded. The man was without doubt quite wealthy. Perhaps only people like that could allow themselves the luxury of being eccentric.

"It's all a matter of time, as I said," he announced again at length, continuing to swing his wooden pendulum. "You truly cannot influence the cause before the effect, but there is another possibility—perhaps you can *after* the effect takes place."

The old man squinted again over the metal rim of his glasses. Watchmakers are like doctors, he thought, self-pityingly and comfortingly: they do not enjoy the privilege of choosing their clients. How would it look if a doctor refused to treat a patient simply because he had strange convictions? Should he now refuse to serve this obviously wealthy quack with a very unusual watch just because of his peculiar ideas? That would be quite against professional ethics, not to mention courtesy. And after all, there was the fee to think of.

"Oh," replied the old man briefly, trying not to sound too surprised.

"Yes," continued the visitor, "although extremely unusual, the idea is actually simple. Going into the past. Going upstream on the river of time, to put it picturesquely. If you returned to the past, you would be able to remove the cause and thereby the effect as well."

"Of course," agreed the watchmaker without hesitation. "Quite simple, as you said, sir. . . . Going back into the past and removing the cause. . . . Nothing easier, so to speak. No cause, no effect. You explained that quite well, sir, quite concisely. . . ."

The stranger did not reply for several moments, and the old man had the unpleasant impression that the unseen eyes were looking at him in suspicion under the hat brim. Did I say something I shouldn't have? he wondered. Maybe I shouldn't have said anything. A man doesn't know how to talk to such people.

"It is not quite as simple as you might think." The visitor's voice seemed to have a bit of reproach in it. "Here's an example:

imagine that you go back to the past and accidentally cause the death of one of your parents—before you were conceived. That would mean that you were never born and could therefore never go into the past and prevent your own conception. And if you were nonetheless born and then you went back to the past . . . and so on. Reductio ad absurdum. A paradox."

The old man stared fixedly at the dark figure before him, suddenly feeling that his hands were sweaty. What was he talking about—causing the death of one of his parents? How could he think of something like that? Was that the sort of thing a gentleman talked to a stranger about, even if he was an eccentric? But what if this person was not some rich eccentric but a madman escaped from a foreign asylum for the mentally ill, who would rob and maybe even kill someone?

Does he intend to attack me? What should I do? How are you supposed to act toward a dangerous lunatic, anyway? Humor him, flatter him? I must not let him know that I realize he is crazy. But they say that madmen can be very bright. . . . If only the ceiling light was on—damn the penny-pinching of the elderly!

"No, there is no solution to the paradox, at least not if you hold to the normal view of time—as a unique river. What has happened cannot be changed at all. The flow of time is like granite in which events are permanently chiseled. Both causes and effects. It is not a palimpsest that you can erase and write on again as many times as you want."

Another short pause ensued, and then the foreigner suddenly stopped the monotonous swinging of his cane. He held it in the hanging position for a moment, as though uncertain what to do with it next, and then with a sharp movement put it under his arm again. All that remained sticking out the front was the figure of the hourglass—a milky spot before a dark background.

"But what if there were not just one time flow, one inscription in granite? If there were several flows—countless, actually? Imagine time not as a single river but as an enormous tree with countless branches, countless forks. Forks appear on those places where you change the past. One branch is the original flow in which a cause produced an effect; that is final—it must remain unchanged, chiseled—but from the other branch both the cause and the effect are removed."

The visitor stopped, as though wanting to check the impression his words had made. The old man was still staring at him fixedly, his mouth half open. In the sudden silence, the muted ticking of the wall clocks rose several octaves.

"And you exist on both forks, in both versions, if we can say it like that. You have a sort of double—more than that, actually—whose course of life differs from yours in some respect. In an essential respect, perhaps. He could be spared the effects of an unpleasant, tragic accident, for example."

The visitor fell silent and the old man started to fidget, feeling that he should say something. However, for several long moments he couldn't think of anything.

"Truly quite clever," he said at last, making an effort so his voice would not tremble. "What an unusual notion! You have figured out something quite brilliant, sir. A tree and then a fork, and a double! Very picturesque, striking, no doubt about it. Something like that certainly would have never crossed my mind."

"Strange. And one would say that you have had both an opportunity and a motive to think about that."

"What are you thinking of, sir? I'm afraid I don't quite understand."

The visitor took the cane in his right hand again and described a rather large arc in front of him.

"Isn't this an opportunity? Look around yourself. You have spent your entire life in the middle of clocks. You are surrounded by chronometers. You are in the very center of time, I might say, in a very privileged position. I cannot believe that in all these past years you have never wondered about the nature of time, how it works, about the peculiarities linked to it. Who else if not you?"

"I am afraid you highly overestimate me, sir. I am just an ordinary watchmaker. Industrious, that is true, yes, and probably good, too, at least that is what they say, but nothing more than an artisan. For me, sir, and please don't hold it against me, time flows as it flows, and if a clock does not measure it as it should, I repair it. I can do that. And that is all. Clocks are here to measure time properly, aren't they?"

"Yes, all right, but what about the motive?"

"Motive, sir?"

The stranger did not continue right away. The watchmaker could almost feel the piercing look of the eyes in the shadow.

"Nothing in your life has ever made you want to go back to the past and change something there? Remove some unforeseen cause that led to adverse effects? Cancel the consequences of some mischance that befell you or someone particularly close to you, someone dear? Has there ever been a man who has never had such a desire?"

Who is this? wondered the watchmaker in fear, suddenly feeling squeezed, as if in a trap. Behind him was a wall, and before him lurched a threatening figure, a voice from the darkness asking inadmissible, impossible questions. His hand unconsciously touched the watch in his vest pocket. This was not some eccentric or madman. Oh, no. Something else was going on here, something unreal, like a dream. Maybe I'm dreaming, he thought with hope. He did not wake up, however, which always happens when this question is asked in a dream.

"What would be the use even if I did want to, sir? It can't be done. I mean, all right, maybe time isn't, as you described, sir, a river, I don't contest that, but that . . . tree . . . with the forks in the branches . . . and the rest. The double . . . but how can a person ever get the chance to change anything? Go back to the past?"

There was no reply from the shadow. The seconds lapsed, long, silent, full of expectation. And then, instead of the stranger, the wall quartet suddenly resounded, breaking off the tense silence and prompting the old man for the first time in his life to jump at the harmonious announcement of the full hour; the very next moment it was transformed into a discordant confusion of grumbling, chirping, chiming, and waltz music.

The visitor remained motionless until the last echo of the grenadier's bass died out and then with a rapid movement placed the top of his cane next to the pocket watch that lay on the lighted felt counter.

"You will look at it, won't you?"

A deep sigh of relief escaped from the old man, as though a heavy load had been taken off his chest. His eager hands finally caught hold of the precious object; they started to turn it over and feel it, examining it as carefully as eyes would.

"Certainly, certainly. Rest assured, sir. Right away. It's not too late. If you would be so kind as to come by in the morning. As soon as I open. It will be ready. At your service, sir. At your service."

The foreigner abruptly turned on his heel, missing the watchmaker's humble bow. The sound of the cloak's stiff fabric merged with the ringing of the bells and the closing of the door. The tall shadow quickly passed in front of the store window and disappeared down the street.

The old man slowly sat down on the chair next to his workbench and put the pocket watch on the rubber surface. He gazed at it for a few moments, turning it over curiously, and then reached to open the lid.

But he did not complete the movement, for he suddenly realized that in the excitement of the moment before, he had forgotten something: he had not given the customer a receipt for the watch. Inexcusable, he thought. That had never happened to him before. All right, he had been disoriented by the visitor's unusual appearance, that strange story, but even so! An unpardonable oversight for a watchmaker who cares about his reputation. What would the foreigner think of him?

He grabbed the receipt book and a pen from the counter and rushed toward the door with stiff movements. Suddenly disturbed, the bells above the door protested sharply. Outside it was cool and windy, a November evening at the foot of a mountain with a great cap of snow already. Shivering for a moment, the watchmaker looked for the visitor down the row of streetlights. But no one was there. Perplexed, he turned and looked in the other direction. Just as empty.

He stayed in front of the shop a bit longer, turning back and forth in disbelief, and then went back inside. Where had he gone? Had a carriage been waiting for him nearby? But no, he hadn't heard anything. Standing at the door a moment, the old man finally shrugged his shoulders. He would apologize to the foreigner for this oversight when he came in the morning. In any case, it would make no difference then. The most important thing was for him to take care of the watch.

He returned to his workbench, interlaced his fingers and cracked his knuckles like a pianist before a performance, and then pulled in the squeaky stool. Before he pressed the clasp to open the lid, he briefly rubbed his fingertips with his thumbs.

His eyes first went to the inner side of the lid. It was an inadvertent, almost automatic act: that was what he always did with the other pocket watch that he kept with him always. There was an engraved inscription there as well that for some reason seemed familiar to him. TO J. FROM Z. was on the gold-plated concave circle, and several long moments had to pass before the old man realized what it was. The shape of the letters, of course! The same large, ornate letters as . . . but how was it possible?

And then there was no more time for ordinary amazement; on top of the wreath woven of twelve elongated Roman numerals the two black hands had started their crazy dance.

II

They seemed to have a will of their own, moving by themselves—but in the wrong direction. They started to turn backward, as though measuring the past, first slowly, so he could follow them, and then faster and faster. The watchmaker instinctively withdrew his hands from the activated watch, but his eyes stayed riveted to its face.

He stared at the big hand as it accelerated and then finally disappeared, transforming into an excited circle; it looked like some sort of film had been placed over the face. The spinning of the small hand was perceptible somewhat longer, and then it, too, melted into an indistinct veil.

This tremendous spinning made the watch tremble on the rubber surface. It suddenly occurred to the old man that he could stop the magic if he closed the cover, but he did not have the courage to touch it. Holding tightly to the edge of the workbench, he felt that the accelerating vibrations of the watch were being transferred to his body: he, too, was shaking as though he had a fever.

And then the trembling stopped, for the watch had detached from the tabletop and started to float a bit above it. Although it was illuminated by the strong lamplight, there was no shadow underneath it, just as though it were transparent. A high, shrill whistle started to sound, almost at the upper threshold of audibility; there was something unsettling in that sound, and the old man wanted to put his hands over his ears but was unable to do so.

As though bewitched, he simply stared at the floating object before him that continued to rise slowly until it reached the height of the old man's eyes. It rested there a few moments, hesitating as though thinking what to do, and then started to spin around its vertical axis. Just as with the hands on the face, the spinning became faster and faster until there soon formed the illusion of a small ball before the watchmaker's bewildered face, his jaw hanging.

As though cut with countless facets, the ball first brightly reflected the light from the lamp on the workbench and then began to radiate its own light as the shrill noise became louder and louder. To the old man's relief, the unbearable sound soon rose above the frequency audible to human ears, leaving behind a muffled, almost palpable silence.

In just a few moments, the dull grayness turned into a reddish glow, then into yellow heat, and finally there was a rapid sequence of shades of white, rushing to the inevitable climax, the act of release. The old man greeted this orgasm of light with wide-open eyes, unable to lower his eyelids; in any case, what could thin, wrinkled skin do against the wild fury of a summer sun less than a foot from his head?

Although he was completely blinded by the explosive flash, he did not feel any pain or even discomfort. The only thing he felt was the strange sensation of being in the middle of an endless emptiness, impenetrable and silent; he made his way through it effortlessly since there was no base or support to hold him back. His body seemed to have completely lost weight and along with it the sense of direction: up might be down or somewhere to the side—he was not able to distinguish anything.

Is this death? he wondered. If it is, then it is very mild, even pleasant. Like a dream. This was not how he had imagined it. Actually, he had not imagined it at all. Who imagines what death looks like, anyway? He had the vague feeling that he should be afraid for some reason, but instead of fear or at least discomfiture, he was filled with childish curiosity. Where was he? Would he remain incorporeal like this forever? Did time exist here? Why couldn't he see or hear anything?

As if in answer to this last question, sounds started to come from a great distance. He did not recognize them at first; they were too muffled and unintelligible. At first they resembled the scraping sound of gravel being rolled by waves on the shore and then the drumming of rain on the leaves in a forest on wet spring evenings. Then something in their rhythm seemed not only recognizable but familiar: the monotonous, regular repetition, harmonious only in the introductory chord and then completely dissonant. . . .

There were seven strokes from the moment he started instinctively to count the hour sounding in four disparate registers. How many had he missed until he understood what it was? Three—or maybe more? There was only one way to find out, although he did not understand why it was important to ascertain this fact. He reached for his vest pocket, forgetting completely that he had become incorporeal. But the pocket was there, real and tangible, as were the vest and his hand—everything was there except the watch that Mary had given him that day. . . . The watch was not there!

How was that possible? Why, a little while ago . . . he looked at his vest in panic, only realizing when he saw it that his sight had returned. He was no longer blinded or surrounded by impenetrable emptiness. He stared at his body for a few moments, filled with disbelief, and then slowly raised his eyes and looked around himself.

He did not notice what was wrong right away. Everything seemed to be normal: things were in their proper places—the workbench which he was still holding convulsively with one hand, the counter covered with green felt, the old-fashioned clothes tree in the corner with his winter coat hanging from it, two armchairs with reddish upholstery and the round coffee table between them with thin, curved legs, the large grandfather clock with its pendulum, the mirror on the opposite wall with the black wrought-iron frame. . . .

Only after he had taken all of it in did he realize where the problem lay: he should not be able to see it all. The only light in the shop was from the small lamp with the green shade in front of him, and the lamplight barely reached the counter. Now, however, he could see everything as clear as daylight. . . .

Day!

Daylight flooded through the large shop window with WATCHMAKER written in an arch of dark blue letters. It was bright and clear, light that in this region was seen only in late spring and during the short summer, certainly not in mid-November. But it was not early winter outside; when a little girl skipped past the shop soon afterward, the watchmaker was perplexed to see that she was wearing a checkered dress with short, ruffled sleeves.

He got up from his workbench, finally taking his numb hand off the edge of it, and took slow, hesitating steps from the counter toward the entrance. When he was in the middle of the shop, out of the corner of his eye he noticed something moving on the right and turned slowly in that direction, encountering his own reflection in the long mirror.

He squinted and stared at his image, refusing to believe what he saw. It was he, without a doubt, but different, changed—rejuvenated. The person returning his look from the glass was not an old man, stooped, his forehead full of wrinkles, gray-haired and balding. He was a young man, barely thirty, standing straight, with smooth skin and thick, dark hair.

He started to touch his face gingerly, afraid that even the lightest pressure could deform it into its former deteriorated grimace like a wax mask. His fingers slid over his mouth, chin, cheeks, trying hard to feel the trickery, but there was no deception: his youthfulness was real—as real as everything else around him seemed to be.

He continued to look at the long-forgotten person in the mirror, while the confusion in him slowly withdrew before the mounting excitement, when suddenly, like a strike of lightning, he had a sensation that he had experienced only a few times before, but never as strongly. The feeling of déjà vu was all encompassing, overwhelming: he had stood in this same place before, looking at himself in the mirror, and the bright summer day had been exactly the same.

Something caught in his throat when he realized what had to happen the next moment. He had no doubt that it would actually happen as he quickly turned around to the entrance. The bells above it started to fly loudly in all directions that same instant. Only she entered like that: like a whirlwind of blond curls, her long, rustling dress, her smile so enchanting with its radiance and cheerfulness. . . .

Mary!

He knew that she would not turn to look at his wide-open eyes, would not notice the paralysis that had come over him, would not hear the thunderous drumming of his heart that filled his ears so much he had the feeling the whole shop was echoing. He knew that she would rush to one of the armchairs and unload the armful of colorful boxes she was carrying.

Her words reverberated in his head a moment before she uttered them, like a reversed echo that precedes the original sound.

"It's so terribly hot. It's even worse down in the town. And crowded. You have no idea. It's as if the whole town were outdoors. You should have come with me. You sit inside too much. It's not good for you. You could have closed the shop today. There are a lot of people here, too. You should see how many carriages there are in the square. Goodness, I'm all sweaty. And I'm terribly thirsty."

She started to rummage impatiently through her rather large handbag made of flowery waterproof fabric; it was always full and now seemed truly inflated. A full minute went by before she finally found what she was looking for. The small box was wrapped in shiny green paper, and the turquoise ribbon had curled ends.

He did not have to open it to find out what was inside. Nevertheless, he did it as inquisitively as he had earlier because he was impelled by the inexorable pressure of déjà vu. After he lifted the cover of the pocket watch and looked at the engraved inscription, he smiled broadly and said the sentence he knew went at that place.

"It's beautiful. Thank you."

He did not have the courage to be more eloquent in his thanks this time, even though he wanted to with all his heart. The object he held in his hand was more to him than just a present from his fiancée: it was an infinitely precious keepsake with which he had never parted in the many years afterward. Even so, the fear prevailed that if he used any other words he would cause an irreparable disturbance and would lose this feeling of déjà vu that was guiding him.

Mary returned his smile and then went up to him, raised herself on tiptoes, and kissed him. It was a light, brief touch of the lips, on the very edge of decorum, considering the time and place, but it made him tremble nonetheless. She suddenly turned toward the door, feeling awkward, to see if anyone was about to enter, and then began to pick up the boxes from the armchair. They were full of the beautiful things she had chosen to look stunning at the upcoming ceremony.

"I'm going to take all of this and get changed. I'm all sweaty and sticky. It's so hot. You should put on something lighter, too. You'll boil. Let's go have lunch at the Golden Jug. What do you say? It's the coolest there right now, in the garden under the linden trees. All this shopping has made me hungry."

She smiled at him again, a special mixture of affection and apology, and then rustled in her whirlwind manner toward the door—to meet the inevitable. The sequence of events stood before him, completely clear, illuminated by the powerful beacon of déjà vu: the wild music of the horse bells briefly muffling the thudding that was rapidly approaching; her hurried departure onto the pavement in front of the shop as the empty carriage wildly jumped on the cobblestones; incautiously crossing the street at the very moment the confused horses without a driver, left too long in the sun and frightened by who knew what, could no longer be stopped; the horrible shock at realizing that there was no way to escape; someone's scream from the other side of the street that seemed to last an eternity; and then the multicolored boxes flying in all directions, opening up and spilling out their insides: an elegant lemon-colored dress with an abundance of lace, a yellow hat with a large brim and a wide ribbon tied in a bow, shoes with large, shiny buckles, a pile of silk undergarments that certainly should not have been displayed like this—the senseless nakedness of death.

"Mary!"

He had to overcome the violent river to utter this word, to scrape off the previous deposit on the palimpsest with his nails, to seize hammer and chisel to write a new inscription on the virgin surface of the granite. The magic of déjà vu shattered at that moment—there was no room for this call; his role had been to remain silent, to merely follow her out with his eyes. Stepping out of the play in which he was unwillingly acting, he was suddenly alone, exposed to the winds of time, without a guide to light his way, but also without the ominous inexorability of the predetermined.

She stopped at the door and turned. "Yes, Joseph?"

He didn't know what to say. He certainly could not start explaining, particularly since he himself barely understood. So he simply went up to her and hugged her, together with her armful of boxes. It was an awkward, hard squeeze, calculated above all to keep her there, not to let her leave. He knew that this could arouse her suspicions since such public outpourings of intimacy were not at all characteristic of him, but he chose the lesser of the two consequences.

"Oh, Joseph, dear, someone might come," she said in a voice whose reproach was only feigned. "Be patient a little longer. . . ."

Somewhere at the top of the street, from the direction of the square, dull thudding could be heard. It approached rapidly, mixing with the clatter of bouncing wheels. The sound was similar to thunder heard backward—from the dying out to the explosion. Mary tried to wriggle out and turn toward the window, but Joseph's embrace held her tightly.

"What was that?" she asked, turning her head to the side.

"Nothing . . . a carriage, probably . . . in a hurry. . . ."

If there was an end to his sentence, it was lost in the deafening stampede, in the strike of lightning. Just like the shadow of a low cloud, the unbridled team whizzed past the watchmaker's shop in a whirlwind of hooves, wheels, manes, empty driver's seat, foamy muzzles, spinning axles, terrified eyes, reins dragging on the ground, sweaty handles—and afterward the thunder resumed its natural course.

"Someone could get hit," said Mary, after Joseph's squeeze finally relaxed. Now he was standing almost penitently next to her, not knowing what to do with his hands that had held her like a vise a moment before.

"Carriage drivers have become so inconsiderate, even arrogant. You should see them down in the town. They tear around like madmen. And how they whip those poor animals. It's terrible."

"No one will get hit, Mary. Not anymore."

She looked at him suspiciously, confused by the changed tone of his voice. He had said it too seriously, as though pronouncing some kind of oath. Even so, as he uttered them, he was aware that they were merely empty words of comfort similar to those said to calm a child the first time he asks about death.

Of course, someone would get hit. The inscription chiseled in granite could not be erased. On another fork of the tree of time he was now running into the street and bending in a convulsion of pain over the unmoving body, while tufts of yellow fluttered all around. He could pretend that this no longer concerned him, that he was now safe on this branch where Mary was standing next to him, the very incarnation of the vibrancy of life, sweaty, laughing, thirsty. But although he did not understand much of it, the realization that both courses were equally real was painfully clear to him.

The clarity with which he remembered the agony he felt as he lifted her off the bloody pavement, heavy from lifelessness, the hopeless insensitivity in which he then plunged for a long time afterward, the slow succession of months and years filled with the deceptive oblivion brought by tedious work, and the lonely, nightmare-filled nights in which the past relentlessly visited him, until that far-off November evening when the bells suddenly rang above the dark door to announce the arrival of the mysterious visitor—that clarity, that hard certainty of memory, was the price he had to pay for this unique privilege that he had been given for who knew what reason: to return to a past time and undo the effects of cruel chance.

He knew that this price did not give him the right to be dissatisfied. On the contrary, the shadow over his restored happiness was a very thin, transparent veil. Nevertheless, in the years that followed, only Mary's intoxicating, infectious cheerfulness managed to dispel the mask of melancholy that periodically, seemingly for no reason, covered Joseph's face.

THE ARTIST

I

HE UNLOCKED THE DOOR AND ENTERED THE ROOM.

If it were not for the bars on the window, it would have looked just like an artist's atelier. The half-open window with the thick drapes and pleated curtains went up almost to the ceiling, letting in an abundance of light during the day. Painted white, the bars were not too conspicuous, but they could not be overlooked. They were not there to prevent anyone from escaping, for this was not a prison, but rather to prevent the final retreat that the mind of the room's occupant might seek from its own darkness.

The room was sparsely furnished. To the right of the window, at a slant, stood a rather large easel spotted with dried streaks of paint and placed on newspapers, yellowed from standing in the sun a long time. Next to the wooden easel was a tall, thin chair with a low back and rungs for feet. Part of the lower half of the wall nearby was covered with mounted shelves that held a disarray of art supplies: mostly squeezed-out tubes of paint, half-empty little bottles of paint thinner, brushes of different sizes, dirty palettes, a bunch of used charcoal sticks and pencils, soiled flannel rags, large sketch pads, a pile of rolled-up canvases, and several cans with bright labels and no lids.

The only light in the room was a reflector light on a short support that was attached to the middle of the ceiling. The narrow beam illuminated the canvas on the easel, reflecting brightly off the fresh layer of paint. The edges of the beam that reached the uncovered floor glistened off the polished parquet.

He headed toward the other side of the room and sat on the end of a narrow bed with a brass frame, next to the door that led to the small bathroom. In addition to the bed, there was only a little white table with drawers: on it was a lamp with a yellow canvas shade, a vase with large-petaled purple flowers, and an old book with a black cover, pink-edged pages, and a wide ribbon bookmark.

His eyes went to the wall across from the window. He could not see well in the semidarkness, but it made no difference. He knew what was there: three paintings in simple gray frames, unevenly arranged. Three scenes of darkness disrupted in the middle by a beam of light: the flickering glow of a torch in the corridor in front of a cell, cone-shaped lamplight illuminating a jumble of old things on an office desk, the green shine of the felt from a watchmaker's counter. And outside the beam, distinct from the surrounding shadows like a concentration of the night, was a spectral figure without a face.

"Good evening, Doctor." She said it softly, with her back turned, sitting on the tall chair. All she had on was a short-sleeved nightgown; her fragile shape could be discerned through its thin, semitransparent fabric. The scene was not stable because the light material trembled and fluttered under the gusts of warm breeze from the window. Her bare feet with their small toes were resting on one of the rungs. The brush in her left hand was making rapid, short strokes about the canvas.

"Good evening, Magdalena. The nurse tells me that you are painting again?"

"Yes."

"Isn't it a bit late for that? Wouldn't it be better for you to go to bed and then get down to work tomorrow morning?"

"I can't. I have to finish the painting as soon as possible."

"You were never in a hurry before."

"Now I have to."

"What for?"

"He was here."

The doctor closed his eyes a moment and drew his fingertips across his forehead. "He came to visit you again?"

"Yes."

"Did he tell you a new story?"

"Yes. The last."

"The last?"

"There will not be any more."

"Oh? Why?"

She did not answer right away. In the silence that descended, distant sounds of the summer night were suddenly audible: the soft rustle of leaves in the tops of the tall trees surrounding the sanatorium, the idle chatter of crickets in the grass, the sharp call of a bird.

"He's leaving."

"Is that why you are in a hurry?"

"Yes. I want him to see how I have painted him. He promised he would come one more time just for that."

"You are going to paint him? He finally showed himself to you?"

"Yes."

"But he has always remained hidden before. You never once saw him during an earlier visit. That is why he has no faces on your paintings. Why the change now?"

"He will still remain hidden."

"How can that be if you paint him?"

Before she replied, she dipped her brush in paint on her palette, mixing colors for several long moments.

"I'll paint him, yes," she said at last, returning the brush to the canvas. "I'll even tell you all about him, if you wish. But you, of course, will not believe me."

"Why do you think that?"

"Because you think I'm crazy." She said it in an even voice, as though stating something ordinary. "My madness conceals him. Better than any darkness."

"You know that we do not use such words here."

"I know. You have other, milder expressions. But that does not change the essence of the matter. There are still bars on my window, and you keep the door locked."

"The bars are there for your own good."

"So I don't lean out too far by accident and fall?"

"Accidents do happen."

She put her head close to the canvas for a moment, engrossed in painting some detail. "So, then, you could believe me."

"I could listen to you and then judge."

"That's fair." She moved back from the easel, taking a look at the detail. "Tell me, what do you think—who is he?"

"How would I know that?"

"But you certainly have some idea," she said, searching again for the proper color on her palette. "I have told you about our meetings. You know his stories."

"Someone very powerful, obviously, since he can do whatever he wants with time."

She found the right color, and her bared left arm started to move quickly before the canvas once again. "The devil?"

For several moments he silently watched her fluttering figure before the painting she was working on.

"He would be a very unusual devil," he said at last. "A devil who does good deeds without any recompense."

"Do you think he did the right thing?"

"Didn't he? Three unhappy people received a unique time gift, as far as I understood."

"And now they are less unhappy?"

"Why, I suppose. They should be. Particularly since they were not asked for anything in return."

"He, too, thought he would make them happy. At first."

"He doesn't think so anymore?"

"No. That is why he is leaving. He discovered that it is truly the work of the devil to fool around with time, even when you have the best of intentions."

"Where did he go wrong?"

She put her palette and brush under the easel, threw back her head, and tried to shake back her long hair. But the curly, auburn locks were too tangled from the long lack of combing.

"Do you remember the story about the astronomer?" Without turning around she pointed her thumb to the right to one of the three paintings on the wall. "If it hadn't been for his nighttime visit before the execution, Lazar would have happily gone to the stake, convinced of how correct, even exalted, his sacrifice would be."

"But it was a mistake. Visiting the future showed him that his sacrifice had no meaning."

"Do you think that people should be freed from their mistakes? Even when it ends up destroying their happiness?"

"Happiness based on illusion, deception?"

"And what happiness isn't?"

He did not know what to reply at first. He felt like a chess player whose opponent has made what seems like a quiet move, but with many traps hidden behind it.

"What is the meaning of happiness if it entails the loss of a life?" he asked at last, in a muffled voice.

"And what is the meaning of life without happiness? That is the impossible choice Lazar was forced to make. With the best intentions. Everything would have been much simpler if he had not seen the future."

"Your visitor did not tell the story to the end. He did not tell you what the astronomer chose."

"He didn't because it made no difference." She stopped a moment. "What would you have chosen if you were in his place?"

A somewhat stronger gust of air from the window raised the hem of the nightgown, revealing slender calves. It brought into the room the abundant smell of grass and certain traces of ozone—the first sign of the storm on the way.

"And what about the professor of paleolinguistics?" he asked, avoiding any reply. He raised his eyes inadvertently to the second painting on the shadowy wall. "She has no reason to regret because chance was thwarted; on the contrary, she went back to paradise."

The artist did not reply at once. She leaned toward the shelf behind the easel, started rummaging around the tubes, selected one and squeezed out a bit of the contents onto her palette. Then she took the flannel rag and wiped off the tips of her fingers.

"To a paradise she was denied, actually. Eva was only an observer in paradise, without the chance to take part in it."

"I didn't have the impression that she felt it was unpleasant being . . . a ghost. Many of those studying the past would be ready to give half their lives, even more, just to be in her position."

She started to put more paint on the canvas. Now she was working on the middle of the painting. "She would have given it all just for one sip of heavenly tea."

"Perhaps, but that was the price she had to pay. There was no other way to find out if everything she had done was accurate."

"But imagine it turned out that she was wrong. That primeval language was quite different from what she thought. It would be a twofold defeat: she would have squandered her past life, and before her would be paradise that she could not enter."

"It doesn't have to be that way. She might prove to have been right."

"Would that be enough comfort for unattainable paradise?"

"But if she didn't return to the past, she would have been left in doubt until the end of her life. This way at least she found out where she stood."

"Isn't it actually uncertainty that makes life possible?" Another quiet move full of hidden menace.

"Your visitor didn't tell you the end of that story, either," he said after a slight hesitation.

"For the same reason as before. It makes no difference what Eva hears when she gets to the fire. The best thing for her would have been to never leave her basement office."

A blue flash suddenly appeared in the upper part of the window, but no thunder was heard. The storm was still a way off. Only the choir of crickets seemed to accelerate its chattering tune.

"The third story differs from the first two in this regard," he said, again turning to the paintings on the wall. "There is no uncertainty in the end."

"No, there isn't, but it still is not a happy end, as it should be."

"It isn't?"

She turned her head toward the window and stared at the darkness.

"It's really sultry," she said. "I can hardly wait for the rain. It's hard to paint in this heat. I'm all sweaty."

He closed his eyes again and started to make little circles on his temples with his fingers. That is where he first felt the change in weather. The dull throbbing there that was slowly spreading to the back of his head indicated that he would spend the night wrestling with a headache.

"It isn't," she continued. "Perhaps it would be if he did not have the memory of the other flow of time in which Mary died."

"But, actually, that was not the memory of something real. It was more the recollection of a bad dream."

"It lasted too long to be just a dream. More than a quarter of a century. Why was it necessary to let Joseph suffer so long? If it was possible to help him, and someone was willing, he should have been put on the other branch of time right after the accident. Only then could it have all looked like a bad dream. This way the scars were too deep and real."

"Why wasn't that done? Did you ask your visitor?"

"Yes, of course."

"And? What did he reply?"

She drew the back of her hand across her forehead. "He said he could not have done otherwise because then the story would not be good. If he had offered his time gift earlier, the hero certainly would have had a better time of it, but then the story would be weaker. The same holds for the other two."

"Strange. I had no idea that the devil cared so much for the literary effect."

She stopped with her brush in midair, not finishing the stroke. "He's no devil, of course. If he were the devil, he wouldn't care at all about what happens to his heroes. And he is abandoning his time stories just so he doesn't transgress against them anymore."

"Well, who is he, then, if he isn't the devil?"

A dull roar finally broke the tranquillity of the summer evening. The storm was about to break. As if by some inaudible order, the crickets suddenly became silent.

"Wasn't it clear from the very beginning? The one who tells stories. The storyteller. The writer."

"The writer?" he repeated obtusely.

"The writer, yes. The writer who accepts responsibility, without which his divine omnipotence becomes just unrestrained diabolic self-will."

"Responsibility toward whom? The heroes of his stories? But they don't exist, they are not real people. There is no reason to burden your conscience because of them."

The thin, pleated curtain on the tall window suddenly billowed out like a white sail. Leaves rustled sharply in the nearby treetops, and the edges of the old newspapers under the easel started to flutter restlessly.

"Do you think so?" she asked briefly, turning her face toward the fresh air coming in from outside.

He pinched the bridge of his nose firmly with his thumb and forefinger. The pain from his temples had moved there, becoming more piercing, burning. This conversation had to be terminated. They had reached a dead end, and it was already quite late. They would continue the next day, when he was rested.

"So the writer is leaving us," he said, getting up slowly from the end of the bed. "There will be no more of his mysterious visits." He headed for the door, and then stopped, remembering something. "By the way, did he tell you how he managed to enter your room and then leave it, in spite of the bars on the window and the locked door? Did he perhaps transfer the omnipotence he has in his stories to reality?"

As soon as he said this, he thought that the question had not been formulated very skillfully. The fatigue and headache were clearly having an effect. She might think he was making fun of her, which would not be good at all for their relationship. It had taken him a long time to get her to leave the cocoon of silence in which she had enclosed herself, to start telling him about the paintings she painted.

"The storyteller cannot transfer his omnipotence to reality," she replied. There was no sound of hurt feelings in her voice. On the contrary, it had a note of joy in it, probably from the excitement of the approaching storm. That often happened among the patients. It was as if they were permeated with the electricity that filled the air. The nurses would have their hands full tonight.

"Then how?"

It started to rain outside. The drops were still scattered, but their heavy drumming indicated that they were large, stormy.

"Don't you get it?" she asked. "There is only one other possibility."

He stared fixedly at her back, over which the thin nightgown was now wrinkling like ripples on the surface of the water. "I don't get it. What possibility?"

"This is not reality. This is also one of his stories."

He stood immobile in the middle of the room. He knew he should say something, that it was expected of him, but he could by no means find the proper words. He was confused not by what she said but by how she said it. That flat voice again, as though it were something quite ordinary.

"I said you wouldn't believe me."

He snapped out of his paralysis. "It's not easy to believe. Would you believe it if you were in my place?"

"Oh, I would, certainly. It's not hard for me. I'm crazy, right? But you aren't. In addition, you are a man of doubt and not of belief. You'll still be suspicious even after you see the proof."

"Proof?"

She laid the palette and brush under the easel again, wiped her hands on the spotted flannel rag, and reached for something in her lap. A moment later she turned around toward him in the tall chair and raised her hand in the air. A yellow gleam danced in the bright reflector beam.

"Where did you get that?" he asked, squinting at the pocket watch.

"From the writer, of course. It is his gift. There is a dedication engraved on the back. Here, take a look."

She held out her hand with the watch, but he did not take it right away. He stared at the golden object on her palm, feeling the hairs bristle on the back of his neck. Everything is really full of static electricity, he thought. As if in reply, everything in the room suddenly flashed a blinding blue. He knew what would follow, but the violent explosion that resounded just a fraction of a second later still made him start.

She did not even blink, as though completely deaf.

"It's only thunder, don't be afraid," she said gently. "Go ahead and take the watch."

He did it hesitantly, timidly. It was heavier than he expected, convex on the top and flat on the bottom. His fingers felt the engraving on the back side, and he turned it over in his hand. The inscription was tiny and curling, calligraphic. Two names above the middle of the circle. Hers, his.

"So that is the name of the writer," he said. It was something between a statement and a question.

She did not reply. The silence that reigned was disturbed only by the downpour from low clouds. Periodic flashes of lightning illuminated the curtain of water just outside the bars. The rain was falling straight down, so the parquet below the window was completely dry. The air in the room was saturated with humidity and some new, pungent smells.

He started to turn the watch in his hand, looking for the latch that would open the lid.

"Are you sure you want to open it?" she asked quietly.

He found the latch but did not touch it. "Shouldn't I?"

"No, if you're not ready for a time gift."

"What kind of time gift could I receive?"

"One that would be able to change your whole life."

He smiled. "Is there something like that for me? There is no execution awaiting me at dawn, neither am I plagued by doubt in my old age as to whether everything I have done has been mistaken, and I don't have the least dark spot in my past that should be removed."

"Oh, it exists for everyone. Even someone crazy like me. It is the final time gift."

"Final?"

"That's right. Tell me, what is the only thing you know for certain about your future?"

He thought for a moment, looking at her suspiciously. "That I will die, if that is what you are thinking of."

"Yes. But you don't know when it will be, tomorrow or many years from now, right? And it is this very ignorance that allows you to suppress the awareness of your own mortality, which would otherwise become an unbearable burden. Not knowing when you will die—that is the main stronghold of life."

The third quiet move. He had the strange impression that an invisible net of checkmate was woven around him and there was no escape. "And if I raised the lid I would find out?"

"You would find out."

The jets of rain were suddenly slanted by the wind. They started to soak the curtains and drapes and made puddles on the floor under the window, reaching all the way to the newspaper under the easel.

He glanced in that direction and then turned toward her again.

"How do you know?"

"Because I opened the watch."

"And you found out when you will die?"

"Yes."

He shook his head slowly. "There's something amiss there. Didn't you say that your . . . writer . . . stopped giving time gifts after the bad experiences he had with them in the first three stories? That he had accepted the responsibility that goes along with omnipotence, that his conscience did not allow him to inflict harm on his heroes? If this is his story, too, as you claim, then he has behaved very badly toward you: you have received the cruelest of all time gifts."

"I received it because I asked for it myself. He fought against giving it to me for a long time."

"But why did you ask for it? Didn't you just say there is no sense in finding out when you will die?"

"My case is special. If he had already imagined me crazy, then I had the right to know how much longer I will have to be like that. It was the least he could do for me, although he did not find it easy."

"What about me?" he asked, rubbing his forehead with his fingers. "I can raise the lid, too. What would be his justification for me if I, too, am a character in his story?"

"You can, yes, but even so you won't do it."

"Why not? What's stopping me?"

"The writer's omnipotence, of course. He won't let you do it."

A smile spread over her face. His thumb started slowly toward the latch of the pocket watch, but the movement was not completed. The knock that suddenly resounded was short, sharp. The tall nurse did not wait to be given permission to enter. She stopped by the door and said quickly, "Ah, you're still here, Doctor. They need you urgently in room forty-three."

He stood there without moving, holding the watch in his open palm. A gust of wind filled the wet curtains again and lifted the newspaper all the way to the easel legs.

"Why, everything is open here," muttered the nurse, rushing

toward the window. "Magdalena, you'll catch cold; put something around your shoulders."

Continuing to smile, the artist slowly took the watch from the doctor's hand.

"Hurry, they're waiting for you," she said gently. "We'll see each other tomorrow. There's time. The story ends here for you, but we will talk about it for some time to come."

II

The nocturnal storm had long since passed, leaving behind dense humidity full of the smell of decay, which would float over the wet soil until the sun rose in a short while. Flattened blades of grass started to straighten up slowly, throwing off the remaining drops of water, but here and there occasional dripping from the leaves bent them to the ground again.

The wind had stopped altogether so that the deep silence just before dawn was disturbed only by short birdcalls. They sounded inquisitive and fearful, like the calls of lost shipwreck victims on the high sea. The spectral echo of these cries remained in the motionless air long after the original sound had died out.

In the vague light of dawn that filled the large window, the white bars no longer stood out against the curtain of darkness. The milky morning light also dulled the sharpness of the reflector beam illuminating the canvas, making it milder, paler. The contours of the few objects in the room seemed to lose their solidity in this new light.

She was still sitting in the tall chair in front of the easel, staring at the canvas before her. She had put a terry-cloth bathrobe the color of a ripe lemon over her nightgown, which made her look even smaller because it was too big: the hem reached almost to the floor, hiding the rungs and her bare feet, and the sleeves hid her hands completely. The cuffs were stained with paint and seemed to merge with the palette and the brush held by invisible fingers.

The enormous face of the pocket watch covered the entire canvas, almost reaching the edge at four points. The corner parts outside this surface were just dark voids that would certainly have been left out if the frame had been circular. Although the thickness of the large watch could have been neglected as well, since it was not part of the area encompassed by the circle, it was still indicated: a barely noticeable reflection of light from some unseen source conjured the gentle curve on the edge.

Compared to the surrounding dark tones, the bright central whiteness almost burned the eyes with its cold glow, sharply emphasizing each detail on it. The twelve numerals were long and thin but not regular. They looked unstable, as though a restless flow of water was passing over them, making them bend and twist. The rippling was more distinct in some places, bending parts of the numbers into senseless shapes or pushing them all the way over the edge of the face.

The four hands were of the same length. The pointed ends reached the perimeter, widening toward the center just like narrow, elongated fern leaves, with a small slit in the middle. The leaves ended in thin stems that met in one point, as though sprouting from the same bud. The opposite hands formed two segments that were at right angles to each other. The vertical pair linked the numbers twelve and six, the horizontal nine and three.

A semitransparent body was resting on these crossed hands, following their shape. Its arms were stretched over the horizontal hands, tightly attached to them. On the palm of each white glove bloomed a large red stain, although there were no nails. The fingers were clenched like claws but did not reach the red blossom.

Red spots also spread on the dark leather shoes, but they looked less conspicuous there. The pain inflicted by the unseen nails was manifested in the unnatural bend of the legs, whose pierced feet were trying in vain to lighten the load of a body without support.

The long cloak was covered at the bottom by a layer of dried mud, depicting clashing brown smudges on the black background. The edges of the cloak were worn and shabby, the hem unsewn in places. The lining was a fiery color and was torn in one place as though it had gotten caught on a thorny bush.

In front of the torso was a dark cane with the top pointing down. It floated vertically without any support, casting a slight shadow over the surrounding whiteness. The ivory hourglass on its end was cracked in the middle. It seemed as though all the golden sand had poured out of this crack, leaving just an empty shell that could no longer measure anything.

The tall hat had a film of fine dust, toning down the black, silky shine. The shape of the derby was ruined by several uneven dents. The wide brim no longer concealed the face because the light came from below, yet it still could not be seen. The emptiness of virgin canvas gaped in the place where it should have been.

She knew she had to finish the painting, that the time of the last story was running out. The missing face was in front of her eyes, perfectly clear in its repentant agony, but the fingers in the sleeve refused to lift the brush.

She had imagined the scene quite differently. She had wanted to paint him doing what he always did during his earlier visits. He would appear soundlessly at the bathroom door, but she would sense his arrival even though she was sitting at the easel with her back turned. He would take the hairbrush with the broad handle of lacquered walnut from the shelf under the mirror in the bathroom. It had stiff and sharp bristles, which is what her tangled hair needed.

He would brush her hair patiently and at length, just as long as it took to tell a story. When he reached the end, her hair would be loose and smooth, and the disorderly curls would be turned into a graceful row of waves. After the very first brushing, she no longer allowed anyone else to brush her hair and did not do it herself, either. She would wash it regularly but would leave it uncombed between stories. The nurses did not try too hard to dissuade her, seeing in her stubborn relentlessness just one of the caprices of their special patients.

It would be a nice painting, perhaps the prettiest of all four. But this still could not be a love story. Or not just that. It came at the end, after the others, linking them into a whole, so that it had to talk about redemption much more than about love. She had realized that necessity but could not understand why redemption had to be ultimately so painful. As she was painting, she herself had felt the torment of the rusty nails piercing the tender tissue of her hands and feet. She had somehow managed to endure the nailing while it was impersonal. Now, however, the crucified person finally had to receive a face.

When she started to make short, rapid strokes on the only unpainted part of the canvas, her eyes glazed over and her lips drew together with a slight tremble. But her hand was sure. From the seemingly unconnected lines, the oval emptiness started to take the shape of the writer's face, distorted by the primordial sin of his art.

And at that moment she understood why the pain was necessary. Without it, he would only be an indifferent god who justified the harm he did with good intentions. If he justified it at all. The suffering he chose brought him redemption by making him identical to those he had transgressed. Without this sacrifice it would not be possible to accept the final responsibility that goes along with writing.

When she had painted the last stroke, she slowly leaned her head backward, and her long, auburn hair spilled down her back. As before, it was a movement of ultimate intimacy, surrendering. She closed her eyes in anticipation. Somewhere outside echoed a protracted, joyous chirp, and the paleness of dawn was edged in pink.

The brush sank into the hair on the crown of her head. The curly locks were too tangled, so the combing out inflicted pain at first, although her radiance disavowed it. The walnut-handled brush made its way slowly, with short strokes, going back a bit whenever the tangle of wild waves offered greater resistance. The lower it got through the agitated sea, the harder and slower was the progress, and at the very bottom the curls were almost matted.

When her hair was finally untangled, the arc of the sun had already pierced the porous green of the treetops. The brush was raised again and this time sank smoothly into luxuriant waves. It made its way easily, straightening out the last rough spots, taming the most obstinate curls. Even though the ends were no longer matted, it stopped there a moment, unwilling to leave the locks that now seemed to have absorbed it. But this moment of hesitation quickly passed. When it slipped out, the curled ends rebounded as though on hidden springs.

She remained immobile, her head thrown back. The slanted morning rays pierced her closed eyelids. The shadow of the bars on the window made a netlike design on the yellow bathrobe. Many twinklings of eternity went by before she finally spoke. And even then the words were almost inaudible, more a movement of the lips than a sound.

"Good-bye, Z."

WRITINGS FROM AN UNBOUND EUROPE

Tsing
Words Are Something Else
DAVID ALBAHARI

City of Ash
EUGENIJUS ALIŠANKA

Skinswaps
ANDREJ BLATNIK

My Family's Role in the World Revolution and Other Prose
BORA ĆOSIĆ

Peltse and Pentameron
VOLODYMYR DIBROVA

The Victory
HENRYK GRYNBERG

The Tango Player
CHRISTOPH HEIN

A Bohemian Youth
JOSEF HIRŠAL

Mocking Desire
DRAGO JANČAR

Balkan Blues: Writing Out of Yugoslavia
JOANNA LABON, ED.

The Loss
VLADIMIR MAKANIN

Compulsory Happiness
NORMAN MANEA

Zenobia
GELLU NAUM

Border State
TÕNU ÕNNEPALU

Rudolf
MARIAN PANKOWSKI

The Houses of Belgrade
The Time of Miracles
BORISLAV PEKIĆ

Merry-Making in Old Russia and Other Stories
The Soul of a Patriot
EVGENY POPOV

Estonian Short Stories
KAJAR PRUUL AND DARLENE REDDAWAY, EDS.

Death and the Dervish
The Fortress
MEŠA SELIMOVIĆ

Materada
FULVIO TOMIZZA

Fording the Stream of Consciousness
In the Jaws of Life and Other Stories
DUBRAVKA UGREŠIĆ

Angel Riding a Beast
LILIANA URSU

Shamara and Other Stories
SVETLANA VASILENKO

Ballad of Descent
MARTIN VOPENKA

The Silk, the Shears and *Marina; or, About Biography*
IRENA VRKLJAN

Time Gifts
ZORAN ŽIVKOVIĆ